MW00717833

DEATH CULT

SAINT TOMMY, NYPD - BOOK 2

DECLAN FINN

DEATH CULT

SAINT TOMMY, NYPD BOOK TWO

By Declan Finn

Published by Silver Empire

https://silverempire.org/

Cover by Steve Beaulieu

For Vanessa.

ACKNOWLEDGMENTS

Before this novel begins, I'd like to thank some people.

First, as always, I would like to thank Silver Empire and the Newquists for publishing this one. More of their input has gone into the creation of this series than possibly anyone else realizes.

I would also like to thank my editor, L. Jagi Lamplighter, for all the input that went into this particular manuscript. She did a fantastic job on this and on *Hell Spawn*, and I suspect she's going to do a great job on *Infernal Affairs*.

I also need to thanks Margaret and Gail Konecsni of Just Write Ink for the first draft edits.

More importantly, I need to thank my wife for the idea of a cult in the first place.

I would like to thank all of the backers behind the Kickstarter page for the series when it launched in September of 2018. It had never occurred to me to launch a Kickstarter, and the faith everyone has in this series is appreciated.

While I think about it, as I write this page, the reviews are already pouring in for *Hell Spawn*. The book isn't even released at this time, and yet there is already talk of awards. My only comment is that I'll take any award my fans want to grace me with. Heck, I'd suggest just looking up the Dragon Awards and throwing my hat into the ring, if you liked *Hell Spawn*.

But the best reward on this job? Is knowing that you, the reader, enjoy the end product.

So, enjoy everyone. Detective Nolan's life isn't going to get any easier. And you get to watch it happen.

Chapter 1

BLOWBACK FROM HELL

I was awoken from sleep to the sounds of my son screaming.

I pulled my service weapon from under my pillow. It wasn't procedure, but I'd had a strange year. My wife Mariel had also drawn her handgun. Large, human shapes appeared in our bedroom doorway. No one had shouted police, nor had they given any indication of who they were.

In short, we shot first and aimed high. The first one went down easily. Mariel's bullet grazed his head, twisting it around. It made his ear the 10 ring, which I hit. The second one took three bullets in the chest and barely lost a step. The fourth bullet made him drop forward.

By this time, we were both on our feet and heading for Jeremy's room. We hadn't practiced this often, but it had been a rough few months, and we were already hardwired.

I wheeled into the doorway of Jeremy's room at a crouch. Mariel was at my back, watching for any other incoming from the stairs.

The man held my ten-year-old son off the ground with one arm, a gun to his head. The man was tall and narrow, swathed in brown leather. His hair was slicked back and slightly mussed from holding my struggling son.

Jeremy held his plushy Ninja Turtle, and seemed to be clutching it with both hands, though I couldn't see his right hand. When we thought he was too old for stuffed animals, he argued that one is never too old for Donatello.

The man cocked his Beretta, and I knew there would be no discussion.

All I said was, "Please don't hurt my family."

The turtle exploded. So did the man's knee. He lurched to one side. Most importantly, his gun went one way, and Jeremy dropped to the floor and rolled out from between me and the perp.

I fired. I didn't shoot to kill since I wanted him alive. (IA liked living perps). I was prepared for this, so I stitched a line of bullets into his gun shoulder. His arm dropped, and the gun tumbled from his fingers. I charged off the floor and caught him with a flying knee. He didn't scream once, even when we crashed into the radiator and his other knee buckled.

I ended up on top of him, but he wasn't discouraged. He threw an uppercut, driving his fist deep into my gut. The impact lifted me off the floor. I'd been lucky, he caught me on the exhale. Otherwise, the fight would have been over. (Trust me. You don't want the wind knocked out of you. Ever) The terrible strength was familiar from the first, and only, supernatural creature I'd battled. It was why I shot for his shoulder joint. I knew firsthand that immobilizing the joint would disable even someone on PCP...Or one possessed by a demon.

With the first hit, I knew I didn't want a second. I jammed the muzzle of my pistol into the crook of my attacker's elbow as he cocked his fist back for another blow. Then I blew his elbow out with a nine-mm jacketed round.

Without a sound, he stopped struggling.

I pushed myself to my feet and backed up, gun ready.

I didn't take my eyes off the invader. "Mariel. Is Jeremy okay?"

"He is. I have him."

I nodded and backed up. I kicked the exploded turtle to one side. I'd worked out plans with my wife and son since the previous monster had tried to kill them both. We just executed scenario 1, variation B. One meant attack in the home. "B" was always a variation with Jeremy held, with his turtle. On my signal, Jeremy was to distract the felon holding him hostage.

The signal was, *Please don't hurt my family*.

At that point, Jeremy was to fire the .22-caliber pistol hidden inside Donatello.

Yes, a pistol for a ten-year-old. It wasn't uncommon for seven-year-olds in some areas to have a .22 rifle and wait a spell before a pistol. But it was mostly a matter of maturity. After Jeremy had directly encountered a demonic infestation, and a possessed serial killer and never throwing the first punch in all the schoolyard fights that followed, despite more than sufficient provocation. He didn't even have nightmares. Think he's mature enough?

We secured the threat, called it in, and got backup (even though village security was probably on it already).

As we went through the motions, one thing kept bugging me. The invader we captured had had his knee, shoulder, and elbow utterly destroyed. I'd slammed into him, adding my weight to his on his knee, and driving the wounded knee into the radiator.

He had never even screamed. Not once.

Chapter 2

CLEAN UP

I waited outside my house as the street once more became a parking lot for police cars. The Glen Oaks Village Office, which ran this little community, had objected to the previous three times that this had happened. It scared the neighbors. It's why this was the last day we would live there. At the very least, we would not have to be threatened with eviction. We were leaving in the morning.

A new car pulled up, parking at a fire hydrant just outside the crime-scene tape. Out strode an older man built like a bean pole. His cheap suit flapped on his thin frame like a scarecrow in a strong wind. He was bald right up the center, with a tonsure of gray hair around the back and sides. His jowls were covered in gray whiskers, as though some grew faster than others. There was a handlebar mustache that was barely on this side of neat. He was too old to be a millennial, but they sure loved his hair. Sorta the way he loved his mustache.

And I worked with him.

"So, Tom, if your place has been shot up twice, do they charge you double safety deposit?" my partner Alex Packard called out as he strolled up my walkway.

I gave him a casual shrug ... as casual as one could be wearing a bathrobe outside in the coldest January on record.

"You forget," I told him, "this is number three. There was MS-13, then the car through the front window, and maybe the Molotov to the front door. So, number four, really. Remember, there's a reason we were 'invited' to leave."

Alex nodded. "Yup. You're hard on the upholstery."

I rolled my eyes. Also, the people of Glen Oaks Village weren't all that friendly. Never mind that I had solved the murder of one of their own residents. Perhaps they just wanted to purge everyone involved in the incident. "Don't ask me, I'm just the target. Take it up with the forces of Hell."

Alex held up his hands. "No thanks. Last time was enough. More than."

I couldn't blame him. Christopher Curran and the legion of nightmares inside of him had come close to wrecking my family, my job, and my city. No one wanted to relive that spot of trouble. That included me, my partner, my wife, my son, the entire NYPD Emergency Services Unit, and the total population of Rikers Island.

I walked back into the house, and Alex came in with me. Uniforms were talking to Mariel and Jeremy. We were still out of earshot when Alex asked, "How'd they get in? Any sign of entry?"

I nodded to the uniforms. "They haven't found anything during the search. Neither have I. Three guys came in, no signs of how." I shrugged. "If these guys succeeded in killing us off, you wouldn't know where to begin." I frowned, thinking it over. "If they could get out as spotlessly as they came in, they could have made me look like a family annihilator."

Alex gave a wrinkled smile and shook his head. "Nah. No one who knew you would buy that for a second. We'd start the investigation immediately by assembling a list of everyone you pissed off. Starting last week, and working backwards. I'd be done compiling the list sometime before I die of natural causes."

I shrugged again as I considered all of the various and sundry people I had rubbed the wrong way during the Curran case. I had made enemies out of at least two movements and the employees of the "Women's Health Corps," and probably the ACLU. When the newspapers made me front page news, I had become fodder for every nutjob with an agenda and too much time on their hands, as well as every anti-cop. It was responsible for one of the three attacks on my home the previous year.

"Probably right."

Alex chuckled. "I guess you'll have plenty of time to move. No way anyone will let you work on this case."

I gave him a small smile. I had thought of that. "We'll see."

Alex nodded to himself, probably working out his own angle on getting me on the case. "Have you checked them out for any identifying marks?"

I had to shake my head. "Didn't get the chance. By the time I had the scene secured and got Mariel and Jeremy out, the unis were pulling up. They took over, and I haven't been allowed near one of them—the bodies or the prisoner."

"Understood."

Alex wandered over into the dining room. Mariel was seated against the wall since the table had already been packed up and away to the new house. Jeremy sprawled out partially on her lap, partially hanging off. He had fallen asleep. I guess after last time, when a demon-possessed serial killer held him at knifepoint, this was relatively boring.

Alex gave a little wave. "Hey, Mariel. How're you doing?"

Mariel gave him a wan smile. "I've been better." She readjusted Jeremy and looked back to the uni, who finished making her notes, gave a quick nod, and wandered off.

Alex grabbed a chair and turned it around so he could straddle it. "So, walk me through it, from the top."

It was over in fifteen minutes after we retold the entire incident about six times. For an incident that took about thirty to sixty seconds, you'd be surprised how long it can take in the retelling. We went over our plans, the rehearsals, the guns. Explaining Jeremy's gun was a problem. It was in my name, and Jeremy had used it. It was less a police issue and more a "New York City hates guns" issue. It wasn't mandatory that every gun had to be locked away unless it was being used, though it often felt like it. I had to make certain to avoid all mention that the three of us considered it "Jeremy's gun" in the reports. Don't ask me to explain the city's hatred of guns. The only good argument against guns in the city came from a visiting Texan who took one look at the crowded city streets and deemed them too unsafe for anyone to fire in self-defense, because if the bullet went through the target, somebody else was going to get hit.

By the time Alex, Mariel, and I were done with that conversation, the meat wagon had arrived. Medical Examiner Holland strolled in. Two bruisers carried a stretcher behind her. If I didn't know any better, I would have said that they were her personal security while she was on the job. But carrying dead weight around all day was probably better than a gym membership for building muscle.

Alex laughed at the stretcher. "You're going to need another one for upstairs."

The uniform looked up from the notepad, confused. "Another two."

I looked over, startled. There had been two shots coming into the bedroom, and I would have sworn that the one in Jeremy's room wasn't that bad. "You have three dead up there?"

The uni arched a brow. "Why? Should there be more?"

"No. But one guy should be alive."

"Really?" She shrugged. "I guess that's why that one guy was handcuffed to the radiator."

I frowned. That last perpetrator hadn't been bleeding excessively, so it made no sense why he died. I looked to Holland. "Sorry, Sinead. More work for you."

She laughed. "They made the mistake of breaking into your place. Their fault, not yours."

They tramped upstairs and came down with the first body within ten minutes. I waved them to a stop. Now that the body was moved from where it fell, I figured it was time to follow through on something Alex mentioned.

Alex and I approached, and Holland nodded. "I thought you'd want a closer look."

"If only to see if I knew the guy."

Holland gave one of her sly smiled. "Oh, there's something here you know."

Holland pulled down the sheet. It was the corpse with the bullet graze on the forehead and one in the ear. He was shirtless, a feature I hadn't seen in the dark. His upper chest was covered with a full artistic rendering of a man getting his heart ripped out and held up to the sun. It was the image of an Aztec ritual of human sacrifice.

It was also one of the many symbols left in blood at two of the crimes scenes of Christopher Curran, while he was possessed by a legion of demons.

I didn't even look away when I asked my partner, "Think I can be on the case *now*, Alex?"

Alex winced. "Maybe. You can replace me. I don't think I want any part of it."

I nodded. I didn't, either. But I didn't think I would have a choice. The demon had promised, that the people who summoned it wouldn't be happy with me. I had no reason to doubt it.

He frowned as the body was covered up and carried away. "You know what? I have a problem."

"I thought you quit drinking." I joked.

"Ha. Ha," Alex stated flatly. He shook his head. "No. I mean that Curran ..." He looked around and made certain that no one was close enough to hear him. His voice dropped to a whisper as he said, "You could smell him coming? Right? But you didn't mention a thing about catching a whiff of these guys. Did they just walk in without you noticing until they were almost on you?"

I nodded with a frown. I had noticed what Alex meant. As part of being a Saint ... *Argh. Wonder Worker. I'm not a saint, I'm not dead yet. Why can't we get better names for these things?* ... One of my abilities was to literally smell evil. I had caught the scent of the demons within Christopher Curran, even before I knew what they were, and even back when they were in a different human being. Like a bloodhound, I could even smell the lingering stench of evil left behind at a crime scene and follow it like a bloodhound. I'd even smelled it coming off a human once, as well as an entire building. But these killers had only given off a faint scent. Being connected to the demon should have caused a smell like a stink bomb.

What fresh Hell is this?

Chapter 3

ADVENTURES IN
INVESTIGATION

Both Alex and I were dressed to impress at the station. Okay, one of us was. I wore a solid black suit, with a police-blue clip-on tie (clip-on because we don't want to be throttled with our own neckwear) and overcoat. Alex's suit was gray and wrinkled, with a skinny brown tie that may have been black in a former life. That life had long since faded.

Alex seemed to have finally calmed down. Along the way, I had helped a woman with her spilled groceries, then helped her walk a block out of the way. I didn't think it was that far out of the way, but Alex seemed to be annoyed about it. (Seriously, it was one block, and the groceries were under twenty pounds.)

We walked into the police station together and had to walk around a stack of glass. I waved to the glazier. "Hey, Eric. This your last day?"

Eric Mahoney, a middle-aged, beefy fellow in a hard hat, scowled. "If I'm lucky. Seriously, what was it that made you people trash all of the glass in the building?"

"The perp got out of control," Alex explained.

"Yeah, yeah, so you guys keep telling me." Eric rolled his eyes and shook his head. "Seriously, one little guy on PCP and he strings himself up? Did he have to work really hard to smash everything? And the vending machine, really? That, too?"

It was another moment I couldn't exactly explain to him. The "junkie" had been a man named Hayes, who had been the first host of the demons within Christopher Curran. It was how the demon had targeted me before jumping into the serial killer.

"Pardon us, Eric." I stepped around the glass, worried about the placement.

At which point, we ran into Internal Affairs.

* * *

THE WORST PART about being me — a living Saint (for lack of a better term) — was hiding it.

Obviously, I don't mean that one has to lie about one's good deeds. That would be idiotic. Just look at Mother Theresa. She didn't hide what she did from day to day. And someone who is truly a saint is humble enough to acknowledge all the flaws of which we are aware, and hence usually do not advertise how good we are— because we know better. We know better, because we know what happens in our heads.

The problematic part of being a "living Saint" (which is oxymoronic, as all Saints are dead by definition) is being a Wonder Worker. Basically, a Wonder Worker has miracles performed through them. You wouldn't think this was a problem … but when you're a law enforcement officer, saying "I healed my wife of the knife wound to the throat" or "I bilocated a copy of myself onto the other side of the barricade" doesn't exactly fit neatly into the average daily DD5 report NYPD officers have to fill out.

And if you have earned enough brownie points to actually be a Wonder Worker, lying isn't a valid option. While being honest is good and virtuous, it is the sort of thing that gives you a first-class ticket to the funny farm.

So when Internal Affairs asks a question where the real answer involves you being in two places at once, it becomes imperative to become creative.

The two IA investigators who had been assigned to my were McNally and Horowitz usually referred to as Statler and Waldorf. Don't ask me which one was supposed to be which.

No, before you get confused, this wasn't even about the event in my home. This wasn't about my family shooting their way out for our own survival. No, this was about the "Rykers' Riot" of two months before.

"How did you get past the police blockade to an island with only one path?"

"I was really fast," was my answer. And I had been. I had to move really fast once my bilocated self-materialized on the other side of the bridge, and the blockade. I didn't want to be caught in the sights of the machineguns on the armored cars.

"Uh huh," McNally huffed. "You going to tell me you just beamed on the other side of the fence?"

I shrugged. "I didn't say that. You did." It was also a fairly good description, too.

"And your wife?" Horowitz asked. "We took a closer look at your body camera video. Christopher Curran slashed her throat open. And yet she didn't die? Care to explain that?"

I shrugged. "I always got the impression that any wound above the collarbone bled profusely. Artery in the arm, the throat, anything in the head. You'll have to ask the paramedics. I'm not a doctor." Notice, I didn't lie. I just stated random facts and hoped they didn't notice I didn't even pretend to offer an explanation.

"How about the blood left at the scene around Curran's body?" McNally asked. "There were at least two massive blood patches on the walls and floor around the body. How did that happen?"

My eyebrow went up. The question was phrased awkwardly, and strangely. Even better, no one had ever requisitioned my DNA for a crime scene. At most, they might have typed it. Unless someone routed through my trash for samples, they didn't have proof that it was *my* blood.

Normally, I wouldn't be too concerned with my blood at the scene. They saw me leaving Rikers Island. Everyone knew I was there. Everyone presumed that I personally put down the riot ... somehow.

The official story involved me going in, breaking up some fights, and disrupting the pace and inertia of the riot. With the major players of the riot put out of commission, the riot dispersed. This was more or less what happened. If you replace "major players of the riot" with "the possessed."

Part of the problem was that I had bilocated ... in the end, I had actually done a four-way split, all but one of me dying in the line of duty. The bodies had faded away, but the blood remained. The two big pools of blood were mine, where I had been impaled with prison bars that had been made into spears. I didn't know if my DNA would be the same coming from a duplicate, but I didn't want to bet one way or another. Hopefully, no one outside of my wife would ever see me without my shirt on – every wound that killed me had stayed on my body as a scar.

"It was a prison riot. I presume there will be blood." Especially since I had to slide through at least one hallway full of it, and none of it was mine.

"How did he die?"

"He fell on some bars, like a tiger trap. All I had to do was step out of his way when he came at me."

"And you got no blood on you? At all?"

I shrugged, not answering. Again, that would require explaining that the body that walked out of Rikers wasn't the body that walked in. Nor had I gotten into any direct fights the last time I bilocated.

Don't worry if you're confused. So was I, and I had been there and done that.

There were more questions, but I managed to stave them off with relative ease. I suspect that I had Help From Above with my little deceptions. While Christopher Curran and his personal demons had made no attempt to be subtle about their rampage, God was more low key.

"I'm surprised you didn't want to ask me about the incident in my home."

McNally smiled. "Just you wait."

"We'll get there," Horowitz said.

* * *

I SAT at my desk in the back corner of the bullpen, planting my back against solid wall. I had no interest in getting taken by surprise. Alex was in on my clean little secret, but I didn't want to share if I could avoid it. I'd prefer to keep it between me and my confessor, but witnessing some of my abilities had dragged Alex and my wife into it. Jeremy just thought I was a superhero, but he'd thought that before I performed miracles. Unfortunately, Enemies from the Other Side also seemed to know about me. Apparently, sending demons back to Hell just allowed them to communicate better via infernal interoffice memos.

"How do you want to play this?" Alex asked. "As much as you'd like a piece of the case, I'm not sure you can. Or should."

He had a point. There was a good reason officer-involved crimes weren't investigated by said officer. I was the target of some obviously bad people and putting me out there was waving a red flag with crosshairs on it.

"I mean, what do we want to say?" Alex continued. "That Curran was really just part of some sort of cult, and now they're out to get you?"

I frowned. "Thing is ... you might not be too far from the truth."

Alex blinked as though I had struck him. "What? You saying there really is one?"

I leaned forward. While I was certain of my fellow officers' apathy towards what I had to say, I didn't want to take the chance of being overheard. "When Curran was gloating, he—it—told me that *it* had been summoned. Which means somebody, an actual person, deliberately brought the demon to Earth."

Alex frowned, then leaned back in his chair. "You have nothing else?"

I shook my head. He leaned back further, lifting the front legs off of the ground. "Well, I see why you didn't follow up with it. I'm not sure there were any leads to follow up with."

I nodded. It was the exact reason why I didn't want to bother. "Until now. With the symbols on the guys who broke in, there should at least be some sort of trail behind them."

Alex held up a hand to slow me down. "Curran was a politically protected monster. Are you sure we want to play these games again?"

I frowned. Considering the lobby behind Christopher Curran and his day job as an abortionist, it wasn't out of the realm of possibility that whoever was behind him had similar protection.

Alex continued. "I mean, if I'm not mistaken, when you get at least four people with demonic symbols everywhere, this counts as a cult. We could call the FBI and give it to them. After all, he was a serial killer, and this cult seems to connect to him. They do serial killers. These guys are at the very least serial killer adjacent. Why not give it to them?"

I nodded to concede his point. "That is all true. Except, who in the FBI do you think could stop them? What if they have another Curran up their sleeves? Unless you know if the FBI has their own squad to handle the occult for real."

Alex said nothing but continued to frown, chewing that one over. We had all hoped that the nightmare was behind us. Unfortunately, I couldn't imagine a situation where anyone else could have handled it without *at least* the exact same knowledge, resources and abilities that we'd had back then. And we were lucky. Maybe the Feds could have brought more manpower to bear. Or perhaps they would have shot Curran, had the demon jump bodies, and we would still be trying to figure out who and what the next perpetrator was.

Alex finally said, "How would you pitch it?"

I sighed. "The tats on our John Does tell us that it's connected to the Curran case, and we were the leads. The fact that Curran's buddies have targeted me just means that the case wasn't actually closed yet, we just didn't know it. They don't take investigators off of an open case just because someone shoots at us."

Alex shook his head. "That could be used against us. You didn't make any friends by the time we were done with the Curran case. There's rocking the boat, and then there's hitting the boat with an iceberg. You, my friend, are an iceberg. And there's a difference between being the target of a lone psycho and being the target of a cult bent on your death. I mean, heck, they could screw up and get me by mistake."

✳ ✳ ✳

OUR LIEUTENANT eventually agreed with me. I think he was less swayed by the "open case" aspect of my argument and more swayed by the political angle that I was already involved. I had already pissed off everyone there was to piss off and having bigwig politicos be angry at one officer was better than being pissed off at the entire precinct.

Alex scoffed and said, "What am I? Chopped liver?"

When our Lieutenant added, "I know they're the wrong tattoos but have you considered MS-13? I'm sure they're still upset at you."

I knew exactly where we were going to go that day.

Chapter 4

REFRESHER COURSE

With our boss' comment about MS-13, I could see our entire day mapped out. It would eventually end at Bellevue, but that was the last stop.

The first stop was to go up the street to Creedmoor mental hospital, meaning that our day was going to be bracketed by insanity on both ends. Though in the case of Creedmoor, I wasn't going to visit an inmate, but one of the ones running the asylum, Father Richard Freeman, OP. He was in his late-forties, skinny, with just a touch of gray at the temples. He wore his black shirt and white collar with a lab coat over it. He was a bit nebbishy, but he had the three PhDs to back it up.

Freeman came to meet me at the front door, trying to make the creepy mental hospital more welcoming than the setting of a horror movie. "We have to stop meeting like this."

I chuckled. "No kidding. You remember my partner, Alex Packard?"

Freeman gave a little nod. "Come up. I'm guessing we're back to business as usual."

Alex scoffed. "If this becomes usual, I'm retiring."

Freeman's office was a walk-in closet, only packed with a desk, three file cabinets, a bookcase, and two chairs. Both chairs were wooden, rickety, and hard to get comfortable in. Even the desk had little room, with a monstrous late-80s computer and monitor on it—I'd offered to buy him a new monitor, but they apparently didn't work with the computer. The shelves were filled with books and papers. He only had two crosses on the shelves.

If he was unhappy with the setup, he never showed it.

This was "the OP Center," suitable for the Order of Preachers, the official name of the Dominican Family—and yes, some are on the Caribbean islands if you Google "Dominican."

Freeman leaned back in his chair and folded his hands over his chest. "What's up this time? I'd heard that Glen Oaks won't have you back now."

I smiled as I sat. "One gunfight too many."

Alex remained standing and barked a laugh. "Probably four."

Freeman frowned. "Understood. What can I help you with?"

Both Alex and I pulled out our phones. Alex showed him a photo of the first tattoo that we saw, of the Aztec heart-carving ritual. I showed Freeman the other pictures that Sinead Holland had sent me after she got all the bodies back to the morgue. They were all of the symbols drawn by Christopher Curran at the murder scenes that he had created while possessed. Some were of the bull-headed demon Moloch, some were eyes within a pyramid, within a six-pointed star;.

Freeman's eyes narrowed. "This isn't good."

"I thought you could give us both a quick refresher on the subject matter," I said. "Especially since Alex wasn't here last time."

Alex scoffed. "I'm not sure I want to know."

Freeman sighed. "Probably not." He tapped my phone. "Moloch, the Carthaginian deity of money. They worshiped him by giving their biggest drain on their wallets into the fire pits—their children." He flipped over to the star, eye, and pyramid. "A symbol of Aleister Crowley, occultist and cult leader. A hundred years dead. Big on summoning demons."

Alex frowned. "This isn't going to get any better, is it?"

Freeman sighed. "Not until it gets worse, I suspect. You know the Aztec connection?"

Alex gave a little shrug. "I have some of the highlights. Cannibals. Wore human skins. Ripped people's hearts out to keep the sun working or something."

Freeman looked from Alex to me and back again. "Are we thinking that this is part of a cult?"

"That's my best bet," I answered. "The demon had some parting words for me when I confronted it in Rikers. It had been summoned. All of them had been summoned." I held up the phone. "These guys seem like the most likely suspects."

"I concur. It's a good thing you're moving. You need better security."

I arched a brow. "I was across the street from the village security office. It didn't stop them. Heck, we don't even know how these guys got in, or how they managed to get that close without me smelling them."

"Yes, I can see that would be a problem. Are you certain that you still have that ability?"

I couldn't honestly tell him what I was. Before I ran into the demon, I'd never noted the smell of evil before. Outside of Rene Ormeno, one of the leaders of MS-13, I'd never had a run-in with someone similar.

"No idea. But then, I don't run into too many people who are pure evil."

Freeman nodded. "How is your phone doing, by the way?"

"Working fine since Rikers Island."

Alex scoffed. "Please. Can we all skip the part of this where we treat the last few months as perfectly rational? We fought a demonic plague on the city, and you're a saint."

"Wonderworker," Freeman and I corrected him.

"Dude, by my count, you fly—"

"It could have been a long jump," I hedged.

"—heal, smell evil, bi-locate, cast out demons—"

"That could have been the exorcism outside," I corrected.

"—and I don't even know what else you do," Alex finished.

I shrugged. "It's not really that big a deal. I don't do it that often. In fact, I haven't done anything that interesting since I came back from Rikers. It's not like the scars healed or anything."

It was Freeman and Alex's turn to go into stereo. "Scars?"

"I have some scars from Rikers that I need to stretch out."

Alex pursed his lips a moment. "Can I see them?"

"You'll have to buy me dinner and flowers first," I deadpanned.

Freeman held up a hand to signal us to stop. "Please, if we can continue?"

Alex and I shrugged.

"One of the things we haven't discussed is that if the demon was raised by this cult, we at least know something we didn't have last time: motive."

I narrowed my eyes at Freeman, then cocked my head. "He told me that his motive was to force me to lose my faith by destroying everything around me." I frowned. "But that really only explains killing little Carol Whelan and Erin. But he wanted me to arrest him and throw him into Rikers. He wanted to stay there and work his way into possessing the prison population. That was the *cult's* goal."

Freeman nodded. "The motive of the demon is that of those who raised it. And the cult has now turned its attention to you, like the demon had."

"They're probably annoyed that you stopped their attack fiend," Alex added. "But here's what I don't get: Where do we find a death cult kicking around?"

Freeman rolled his eyes. "You want to talk about Moloch and death cults? Here, let me give you a list of examples. Where would you like to start?" He turned in his chair and grabbed a book off of the shelf. The title was *Culture of Death*. "Would you like to start with how Oregon health insurance won't pay for a heart transplant, but they will pay for your doctor to help you kill yourself."

"Supreme Court Justice Ginsburg said not too far back that abortion was 'For people we don't want any more of.'"

Freeman's topic jumped at random again. "Here's a great one.

Doctors tell a newborn baby's parents that the baby is going to die in a few years, so the doctors were going to let him die now. Because."

I shrugged. "Don't forget when the UK decided that a little boy had to stay in Britain so he could be starved to death and taken off of life support, because he would have survived if he went to Italy—and survival 'wasn't in the boy's best interest,' so the parents were deemed a flight risk while they watched their son die in front of them."

Packard shrugged. "Okay, fine then. So why not start with President LaBitch again? Curran was one of her creatures. If we gotta start somewhere, why not her? What's the worst she could do? Blow up our car again?"

Chapter 5

TEMPLE OF DEATH

The first time we drove into the city to meet with Women's Health Corps President, Joanna LaObliger, we drove away from the meeting with no answers, and I felt the need to take a shower. I drove to the nearest church, ducked into confession, and our car promptly blew up. So far, no one had been arrested for that particular attempt on our lives. To be honest, given how many people were actively trying to murder us at the time—such as MS-13 and the demon—we shouldn't assume that the WHC had tried to kill us. Though when we had a conversation with her later in the DA's office, she certainly cooperated fairly quickly.

I knew for certain that my faith made the WHC people twitchy. For all I knew, the bomb could have been planted by any employee worried that we'd discover a random secret or sideline.

The Margaret Sanger Health Center looked more like a bunker than anything to do with "health"—it was ugly brown concrete, but at least the windows opened. There was a bright pink banner outside that read "Health care happens here."

I slid into park in front of a fire hydrant. I took our police placard and placed it on the dashboard so we couldn't be towed.

"How do you want to play this?" I asked.

"Hit them hard, hit them fast," he answered. "These people tried to blow us up. I object to that."

"Actually, I meant if one of us should stay with the car this time."

Alex looked at me closely. "Is this about the smell?"

I winced. I had been trying not to think about the last time I walked into the building. The scent of evil had nearly knocked me over. It was worse than the MS-13 leader, and as bad as the demon. It was like a Southern body farm that had been left unattended for summer. I had to work not to vomit. I had explained it away last time as a genetic quirk. Alex had remembered and put it together. Last time, I decided that if God granted me these gifts, then I had to stand up and roll with it. That hadn't changed.

"Actually, I was worried about someone trying to blow up our car again."

"Oh. Yeah. That would be a problem." He frowned, then reached forward and grabbed the radio. He called in, gave our call sign and our position, and asked for the nearest available officer to come and meet us.

Within two minutes, we had a police officer on a bicycle skid to a stop next to us. We explained the situation, and he gave us a nod. "Nothing goes boom today."

"Thanks."

I turned towards the building, nearly running into a pregnant woman. She was a pale brunette who was only slightly pregnant (slightly referring to the distention of the belly. It was either a small baby bump or the oddest beer belly ever). "Sorry, ma'am."

She blinked. She looked at me, confused, as though nothing had happened. After trying to meet her eye for a moment and saw that they wandered all over the place, I took her by the shoulders, placed her on the hood of our car and smiled.

"Hi, ma'am, are you okay?"

She blinked, clearing her eyes. "I'm sorry. I'm not feeling very well."

I looked down and decided it wasn't a beer belly. "Well, you have to be careful and take all the prenatal medications."

"What medications? I wasn't told I had to do anything different until the baby was born."

It took me a moment for this to sink in. I glanced over my shoulder at the building. "You weren't coming here for care of the baby, were you?"

"I have an appointment in a few minutes. Why?"

This was the moment where I had to resist the urge to open the trunk of the car, grab the long gun inside and kick open the doors of the Women's Health Corps with a witty 80s movie line like "And I'm all out of Bubble Gum."

Instead, we spent the next fifteen minutes together. I walked her through everything I remembered about Mariel being pregnant with Jeremy while one of the bike cops played gofer.

Alex patiently waited for me to be done with her – her name was Melissa, she was 21, married, and desired to keep her baby, the latter being something I suspected the WHC to be firmly against.

When she was more stable, Melissa waved us away and told us to go to work. I called up the contact information of Mariel's doctor and gave it to her before we did.

I grabbed the door, held my breath, and pulled it open. It stank just as badly as before. I had not lost the knack of smelling evil after all. Yay, me.

I let out the breath slowly and committed to sticking to shallow breaths until I could get used to the smell. With a normal scent, we smell it for a bit, and then our nose kind of goes numb to that scent and one really stops smelling it unless it is brought to your attention. No such luck for evil. The last time I was in the building, I smelled it at full strength all the time.

Alex identified us at the front desk. "Hello. I'm Detective Packard; this is Detective Nolan. Tell President LaObliger that we want to talk to her."

As we went through the building, unlike last time, I kept praying continuously. Though like the last time, I couldn't narrow down where the smell came from. Was it the abortions themselves? Or the people performing them?

And once more, when I noted a massive spike in the stench, was as I walked into the office of the President, Joanna LaObliger. She was tall, bone-thin, Botoxed, and her hair was dyed purple. If chins could kill, she'd be arrested for possessing a lethal weapon, and her nose long and sharp enough to use as a farm implement.

Given our last conversation with Joanna LaObliger, the first thing I did before we left our precinct boundaries was to stop and get a body camera. Recording on my phone worked well enough the last time, but now that we both knew just how hostile this was going to be, I wasn't going to take any chances. Besides, killing babies was LaObliger's day job. Perhaps lying to the police would be effortless in comparison... Yes, I know that's a gross exaggeration, but I couldn't pinpoint what about her was evil, I could only smell it. Was she a sociopath in a business suit, a "snake in a suit" that would be evil, even if she were running a bakery? Was it the job she had or the person she was?

"What do you two want now?" she barked as soon as she saw us.

"So glad you remember us," Alex snarked as he tossed himself into one of the guest chairs. I was surprised it didn't crack, but he certainly gave it his best attempt.

"You ruined a whole day of my life in September. It's hard to forget."

I sighed and shook my head. On the one hand, I knew that there was no real need to be politic, unlike last time. On the other, letting Alex and LaObliger snipe at each other would eat up our time and her tolerance. I wanted some questions answered before she lawyered up.

"Listen, Miss LaObliger," I began. Last time she had wanted to be called Doctor—she wasn't one. I had settled for "President." Now, I wasn't worried about showing all due respect; if I matched her attitude towards me, I could be investigated by IA. Again. "You recall Christopher Curran, don't you?"

"Of course I do. One of our doctors that you railroaded with murder charges."

I held up a finger. "One, he wasn't a doctor." A second finger. "He was the murderer who nearly killed my wife and child. We have him on video. Now, did Curran have any close friends or relationships within the WHC?" I couldn't call her business the "Women's Health Corps" with a straight face.

"No," she answered. "He was a loner. He did his job and went home."

"To his basement full of dead kids," Alex drawled.

"I told you this last time," she sniped.

"Only because we hauled you down to the DA's office in cuffs," he shot back.

"President LaObliger," I started again, straining to keep cool. Between her attitude and the hellish stench coming off of her, I had trouble keeping it together. I already felt ill. I needed to get through it and get out. "Christopher Curran left markings behind at his crime scenes. Last night, men wearing these same markings attempted to kill someone who worked on the case that indicted him. This implies he was part of a larger organization. One that is interested in getting payback. Are you saying that you know of no one who fits that profile?"

She crossed her arms in front of her in a huff. "Of course not."

"Has there been anyone in the WFC who may have expressed an interest in Curran's activities?"

"Everyone is on alert against your persecution," she growled. "We all saw what you did to him in Rikers. Could you have murdered him in a more medieval fashion? Impaling him? Why not crucify him?"

Alex scoffed. "Too good for him."

I didn't roll my eyes, sigh, or anything else I was tempted to do. "Are you a fan of anthropology?"

That caught her. She flinched, taken aback at the change of topics. "What do you mean?"

"Do you or anyone you know possess an interest in ancient cultures or religion? Carthaginian? Aztec? Druidic? Anything like that?"

"Cult of Moloch," Alex snarked. "After all, he is full of bull, making him perfect for politicians."

LaObliger snarled. "No. I don't. And no one else I know does, either."

"Is that it?"

"Of course," she sneered. "Now get out. It was offensive enough you came here at all. Now this? This is intolerable. You can be assured that Mayor Hoynes will hear of this harassment."

Alex and I exchanged a glance. I tried not to laugh. Alex snickered. Mayor Hoynes was an anomaly for New York City in that he was a semi-(big-L) Libertarian. He was less anomalous in that he was a loudmouth who wouldn't know how to shut up if the city depended on it. But seeing Hoynes involved at street-level policing was absurd.

While, as a left-Libertarian, Hoynes was all for abortion on demand, he also made a point of staying out of the way... but like all big-L Libertarians, that didn't stop Hoynes from opening his mouth at every available opportunity. It was a problem of the Libertarian. While I'm an NYPD Detective, I was a small-l libertarian—I believed in letting almost every available virtue *and* vice be available, as long as it didn't hurt anyone else. I could *politically* justify outlawing abortion because it denied life to a child, interfering in his or her freedom. Big-Ls, however, like Hoynes, preached "freedom to think for yourself," then browbeat and bullied anyone who disagreed with him.

Okay, on second thought, maybe Hoynes would *be stupid enough to interject himself into the situation.*

"Hate to tell you," I said aloud, "we do our job without influence, fear, or favor. That's the mayor's office or the *New York Times*. It doesn't matter. You're just going to have to rely on your innocence to get you through."

I can only presume that there was direct intervention by God Himself to allow me to make *that* statement with a straight face.

LaObliger narrowed her eyes at me. I had seen more humanity in the eyes of a shark. "There's no such thing as innocence, Detective Nolan," she said at a low, even tone. "That would imply that there is a right and wrong, good and evil. There isn't one. There is only what I want, what you want, and who can get it. Laws are merely an exercise in the powerful subjugating the weak. You can't touch someone at my level. Or anyone in government above the rank of Lieutenant. Trying to enforce the law on *anyone* is just acting as a tool of your betters. If you truly believe otherwise, then you're more ignorant than I could possibly fathom. Get out of my office. Now. Get out of my building. And stay out of my way, lest you find yourself stepped on like the bug you are."

I nodded slowly, my features set in a semblance of thoughtfulness. It was the best way I could avoid looking ill. I almost thanked her for the belligerence. If she had been helpful and kept us there to have an extended discussion, I most likely would have been sick all over her office.

I stood, ready to go. "You know, LaObliger, I don't think I've ever heard someone talk like that outside of the movies. Funny thing, though? I only ever heard a monologue like that delivered by the bad guys. And they always end up losing. Good day, Miss LaObliger."

She stood so suddenly that I was worried that she was going to leap over the desk and assault us. It would have been strange, but no stranger than fighting demons. "The Mayor *will* hear from me, Nolan," she screeched like a harpy. "Just you wait!"

As we made good time down the hall, Alex told me, "Wow, and I thought I was cynical. She could etch chrome with her attitude. And that's just her personality."

I sighed, which was a bad move since that meant I had to take one extra breath. "I know. I'm not a fan."

Alex gave me a sidelong look. "You think she's guilty. Don't you?"

I shrugged. "Of something? Certainly. But of what? Can you see her ordering an assassination? Really?"

"No," Alex answered. "But I can see her doing someone in herself."

"Also my problem. I can't reconcile it." I breathed heavier as I talked and walked and felt ill. "Let's get out of here. You never know who might be listening."

As we walked down the hall to the elevator, rode it down, and walked out to the front doors, we said nothing.

Alex chuckled as we passed through the front doors and onto the sidewalk. "You never know who might be listening? Are you paranoid now?'

I took a deep refreshing breath, outside of the smell of nightmares inside. "It's not paranoia if people really are out to get me."

Alex smirked. "Tell it to the DSM."

I gave him a sidelong look. "Depending on which year's edition you read, belief in God is a disease requiring talk therapy. Some 'diseases' get there to be reimbursable under health insurance, like smoking cessation. 'Being a teenager' is a medical condition they can prescribe drugs for."

He cackled. "You mean it isn't?"

I groaned. "Get in the car."

This time, the car did not blow up on us. I thanked the bicyclist and drove off.

It was time for our next and final stop, which was the Bellevue Psychiatric Center. It was time I finally came face to face once more with Rene Ormeno of MS-13.

Chapter 6

JOURNEY INTO MADNESS

The DEA had wanted Rene Ormeno as a leader of the vile and vicious MS-13. The DEA wasn't the only one, but it got first dibs. He had been wanted on charges from possession with intent to distribute to human trafficking, and nearly everything in-between. It wasn't so much a criminal organization as a religion that worshiped evil. And the DEA thought that flipping him would have been the solution to a great many problems. That was before Ormeno had been temporarily possessed by one of the legion within Christopher Curran. Now he was a gibbering lunatic inside Bellevue's psychiatric ward, a guest of the city.

Do I have to say that the DEA wasn't happy with New York City? They wanted someone to leverage. They got a delusional freak. But given that everything was coming back to haunt us, and Alex and I had been pointed in the direction of MS-13 by our boss, we had a reason to be there, and we were in the neighborhood. So we were going to try to get information out of him.

I hadn't seen Ormeno since we had gone a few rounds in Rikers. He had nearly killed me, and I had barely gotten away.

Now, he was wrapped in a straight jacket, locked in a padded cell. Before we walked in, his jacket had to be strapped to the wall. He thrashed against the jacket and the straps alternately, unable to concede that he was in for the long haul. His unintelligible screams had echoed down the hallway before we even stepped off of the elevator.

But more pressing and horrific than the screams was the smell of evil that came from down the hallway. I couldn't gauge the directionality of the smell, but I presumed it was only from Ormeno. It was the culmination of every rotting corpse at a body farm, compounded and compressed into one wave of corruption and filth. It didn't make my eyes water the way a physical scent would, but the impact was almost a physical slap to the face. I was grateful that my stomach was empty, but I still felt the urge to vomit.

One of the orderlies met us at the elevator. He was big, burly, and Sikh. He had a black eye and disjointed nose and looked like he had barely won a fight. He shook my hand with an iron grip that had a practiced gentility to it, as though he knew his own strength and held back.

"You're here for Ormeno?" he asked, raising his voice to be heard over the screaming.

I nodded, then looked to his black eye. "How'd you get the shiner?"

He shrugged, as though it were just another on the job incident. "From Ormeno."

Alex cringed next to me. "Geez. Really? You guys let him out of his restraints?"

The orderly shook his head. "Nope. This was when he was strapped down. We haven't let him out of restraints in months."

Alex looked at me and calmly said, "I think I'll stay outside his cell."

The orderly shrugged. "No idea what you think you're gonna get out of him. He's been incoherent and ranting since you left him here. The cops, I mean."

I nodded. "He may be a lead on a case. So we'll at least try to get something out of him. Is he always in isolation?"

The orderly nodded.

"Always," he had to call out over the wailing and gnashing of teeth. "We keep the cells on either side of him empty when we can. He makes his neighbors worse whenever he has any. It's why he's got a corner apartment. Next time you get a guy like him, I suggest you put him down like it the rabid dog he is."

I rolled my eyes and gave an amused scoff. I couldn't even take that seriously. Walking into a cell and shooting someone in the head was just so…1920s Chicago. "Sorry. We're not in the assassination business, no matter how many headlines and op-ed pieces say otherwise."

The orderly shrugged and led us to the back corner cell. The wails of the damned weren't muted by the door.

"Scream if you need me." He unlocked the cell and stepped away, leaving us.

Alex just gave me a look. "After you."

"Gee. Thanks." I grabbed the handle and pushed it open. The wave of evil's stench hit me at full force. Ormeno may have been mad, but he was still evil.

The screaming suddenly stopped.

Rene Ormeno was bald and tattooed all over his face and scalp. He had twisted himself up in the straps so badly, he hung sideways off the back wall of his cell. But he relaxed as he fell off the wall onto his feet. Ormeno slowly turned to face us.

"Why, hello, Detective Nolan." Ormena's voice came out in a rasp, almost a hiss. "What brings you and your partner here?"

He sounded an awful lot like Christopher Curran. I heard Alex swallow behind me. Obviously, he caught it, too. I couldn't begin to guess at what that meant. Was Rene still possessed? If that were the case, why hadn't he broken out weeks ago? And if he were still possessed, did that mean that the demon that possessed him had lain dormant? Were the people we thought had been exorcized were still possessed, and Rikers was about to explode?

All of this went through my brain in an instant. I kept myself calm and my tone even. "We came to talk to Rene Ormeno," I said. "Is he in? Or am I speaking to Someone Else?"

Ormeno's eyes narrowed, amused. "I'm here, Detective. The brief guest in my soul had left an indelible impression. It was…" He gave a shadow of a smile. "Overwhelming. Overpowering. But I'm happy you're here. It's been a while since I've chattered with someone. Have they come for you yet? The cult of death?"

I finally looked back at Alex. He had stayed at the threshold, but gave me a look. A death cult was not a terrible name for what we were looking into.

Ormeno noted our faces and continued. "Oh, good. They've been by. So happy to see that the boys are keeping busy. It wasn't the warlock, or you'd be dead already. Pity."

Warlock? Well, then, this is gonna hurt. "What do you know?"

Ormeno laughed. His voice was low and amused. "Oh, nothing much. Whispers in the dark. Gossip from the lower depths. Water cooler chatter left behind by my house guest."

I winced. I tried to imagine not only being possessed by pure evil but remembering what was in its mind. I'm not sure describing it as pure Hell would have been putting it strongly enough. But then again, the demon inside Ormeno had driven him mad…

"But don't worry," he added. "They'll find you. Soon enough. Do think of me when they send you to join Mister Curran, Detective."

I studied Ormeno closely. This wasn't the gibbering nut I'd been told about. His screams stopped when I touched the handle. Either he'd been faking and knew I was coming, or else …

"How would you know?" I asked. "If you're only lucid when I'm here?" It was a guess on my part, but it wouldn't surprise me.

Oh, let's face it, I thought, *it's God's presence that's doing it to him. Not mine. I just brought Him along for the ride in a more manifest version. I guess.*

Guess or not, Oremno's eyes flickered. I'd hit a nerve. But the smile never wavered. "I'll get an exoneration from the mayor if all else fails."

Wow, he really is deranged. He couldn't tell the difference between a governor and a mayor. I guess I can only cure demonic-created insanity.

"But then," Ormeno continued, "you may not last long enough for the Cult of Death to get you. My men may not be so generous."

I'm certain that Alex would have rushed to mouth off at him, but gunshots interrupted my thought.

Ormeno's smile flickered. "Too late."

Chapter 7

RUNNING THE ASYLUM

I rushed out of Rene Ormeno's padded cell, and he started screaming as soon as I passed the threshold. The gunshots were obviously from another floor, but they were coming close. Apparently, no one knew exactly where Ormeno had been placed, so his MS-13 buddies were happy to wage war on the entire hospital. It was a large building, and MS-13 never cared about being discriminate with their ammunition. They'd slaughter anyone in their way, everyone in the hospital, and everyone who answered the 9-1-1 call.

"Okay, Alex, call the elevator. Orderly! What's your name."

The big Indian orderly snapped out of his reverie at the gunshots to turn his attention to me. "Tak, sir."

I scoffed, but I didn't slow down. "I'm not a sir, I work for a living. I'm Tom. We're going to go down to meet the attackers. You'll have to hole up here. You said the cell next to Ormeno is empty. Try hiding there. Hopefully, you won't need it."

Tak nodded slowly. "Why?"

I couldn't think of another way to say it. "Because if you need to hide, we'll be dead."

"Tommy, we're up," Alex called.

I looked over, and he had his ear pressed to the elevator door, gun held low at his side. I reached for my sidearm and rushed over. He backed away from the door, gun poised at the elevator. I slid to a stop next to him and readied my weapon.

The elevator opened. It was empty.

I darted forward into the elevator, and hit the alarm button, locking it in place. "We've got them right where we want them."

Alex tilted his head to one side. "Which is where? In the staircase?"

"Where we can engage them."

Alex sighed. "You're going to get me shot. I just know it."

* * *

ALEX and I went down a stairwell each. It would've been counterproductive if we went down one set of stairs as MS-13 came up the other. We kept in contact with Bluetooth earpieces and cell phones. We checked each floor as one and moved down. We went down four and a half floors when I was hit with the stench of evil. The smell caught me while I was still on the landing.

"Alex!" I whispered harshly. "The next floor is the one we want. I can smell them."

I wheeled around the stairs, heading down, and heard voices on the other side of the door for the landing. I had seconds to figure something out. I kept coming down the stairs, and I was five up from the landing when the door opened. The gunmen were not even looking my way when they opened the door.

In the two seconds from when the smell hit me, I had time to decide how to engage. Shooting them was easy, but my semiautomatic gunfire was also a great way to let everyone else with them know that Alex and I were on scene.

I leaped for them from the step. My left hand caught the open door at the corner and slammed it on the entire group as they came through the open doorway. Three of them were smashed together between the door and the frame. The AK-47 of the leader was squished between two of them. The leader had poor trigger discipline, because his rifle went off in a spray of bullets, cutting through two of his own men like a buzz saw. I clapped the side of my gun against the ear of the man caught in the middle. It shook him but didn't drop him.

The AK ran dry, leaving me only three men. I targeted the man in the middle again, stomping against the side of his knee, bending it in a way that nature had not intended. He screamed and fell from between the other two men. The leader tried to bring the AK to bear, but I had still been putting pressure on the door, so the muzzle of his weapon drove into the stomach of his friend against the door frame... This was even more unfortunate when you consider that the rifle had a bayonet on the end.

I chopped the top of my gun barrel against the leader's throat. He gagged, and I grabbed him by the back of his head and slammed his skull into that of his dying friend, head-butting each other. I stabbed my gun into the side of his neck four times. The leader dropped like a sack of rocks, and his friend with the bayonet joined him on the floor. I flicked my gun from thug to thug, making sure no one was getting up to cause trouble. The one with the broken knee was gasping in pain. I stepped over his dying friends and stomped the sole of my foot into his face, silencing him. They were all staying down.

"Alex," I said quietly into my Bluetooth, "they're all on the tenth floor. Be ready for them. I got five already. No idea how many are left."

I stepped into the hall.

"I'm on your nine," Alex whispered in my ear.

I inhaled, focusing on the smells around me. I caught the scents of evil, plural. I could tell how many men were up on the floor. It was like walking into a body farm, but you can tell the ones who were composted versus the ones who had been left in sweltering heat.

"Alex, we may have as many as thirty."

"Confirmed."

I frowned. I didn't like the setup. The hall to my left was dark and empty. The hall in front of me was made of solid offices from one end to the other. There was plenty of cover, only if the offices were all unlocked. The walls were riddled with bullet holes. There were three bodies on the floor and high-velocity spatter. One body was sprawled on the floor, holes in her back. File cabinets were knocked over and enough papers on the floor to be a carpet.

My first thought was to wait and see if we could set a trap for the gunmen at the stairs. They'd have to come for us.

Then another burst of automatic fire echoed down the hall.

I gestured down the hall with two fingers. "No time to wait. Alex, go down the right. I'll take straight ahead. Maybe we can catch them in the middle."

Alex groaned. "Can't we just take one of the AKs?"

"Only if you want to go into a shootout with a weapon you've never handled before."

I charged ahead. I hopped over a cabinet and was lucky I didn't slip on a pile of papers. I had to slide under a tall bookcase that had been diagonally blocking the hallway. The smell of evil became stronger as I dove ahead.

Then it hit me hard. I dropped to one knee and wheeled right. It was an open door, an MS-13 killer with a knife held against a doctor's neck. I didn't even give a warning but fired three times – twice to the ribs, and one in the neck or head. I couldn't tell before he dropped. I waved to the doctor to stay put. Now that I had fired my weapon, the gunmen would be alerted to something amiss. I didn't want a civilian shot in the back if MS-13 came out and took shots at me.

I dashed away, hoping to get to the dogleg in the hall before MS-13 did. Now that I knew I could smell out different scents of evil, I had an edge. I also had God on my side ... which was nice, but I didn't think God would save me if I let Him do all the work.

I skidded to a stop at the corner. I quickly sneaked a quick peek. The bulk of MS-13s forces were ahead of me, going door to door. They apparently hadn't heard my gunfire over the sound of all of their own. I could technically start shooting them in the back (No, I had no compunction against it. They were killing innocent people and laughing about it), but I'd have to reload before I got even half of them. And yes, I did have the bullets.

I needed a distraction, at least.

I swapped out for a fresh magazine. I would have to have as many bullets as possible as fast as possible. "Alex, have you run into any of them yet?"

I heard Alex's breathing heavy in my ear. He said, "Not yet. Turning a corner."

I frowned, thinking over the odds. "This is going to be messy. I think we can bottle them in. I'm going to engage."

"You're gonna *what*?" Incredulous barely began to describe my partner's tone. It was as though I had told him that Cookie Monster was my backup, and he was high on thin mints.

I let out a breath. Then I spotted my chance. I took a step forward and pulled the fire alarm.

The sprinklers immediately opened up and poured down on everyone. The alarm made an unholy din. I wheeled around and opened fire. I went through fifteen rounds in less than half as many seconds—all of it was point and click, and I refused to slow down. I wheeled back quickly and refreshed the magazine. I dropped to one knee as I peeked out. The attackers were still checking for cover from the downpour. One idiot opened up on the sprinklers with his AK, flooding the hall even more.

I took at least a moment to aim this time, taking a second for each bullet. No one had taken cover yet, and we were at relatively close range. If there was even thirty feet between us, I'd have been surprised.

It was twenty seconds, and I shot thirty people. Five MS-13 guys were still up, and they spotted me. I wheeled back as they opened up with full automatic fire. I slid further away as the bullets punched through the wall.

Single fire rounds came from down the hallway. I could only guess that Alex had come through. The automatic fire stopped as I reloaded. I flattened against the floor and slid out around the corner. Two of the remaining five were down. Two more fired at Alex, and one fired at where I had been—not where I was. The bullets went over my head as I returned fire. The shooter took five to the chest and abdomen, falling backwards, and spraying the rest of his magazine into the ceiling.

The remaining two gunmen were distracted. I shot one, and Alex got the other.

As I lay on the floor in a puddle of water and shell castings, the alarm blaring in my ears, I studied the hall of bodies. None of the gunmen were getting up, and everyone else had either fled or stayed in their offices.

I pushed myself to my feet. I was wet, tired, and felt like a wreck.

Alex wandered towards me, holstering his gun. He kicked the guns clear from the fallen as he walked along. "You know, if God's on your side, then why does He keep dropping us in the soup like this?"

I shrugged. "I guess He wants someone on scene to handle it."

"Maybe He could pick someone else."

I chuckled. "Maybe. But hey, at least we know we're on the right track after talking to Ormeno."

Alex scoffed. "Yeah, assuming *he's* just not completely around the bend and just spouts out whatever BS comes into his head."

As per policy, Alex and I were taken aside and interviewed. We were interviewed separately, together and grilled endlessly on what we did and didn't do. Thankfully, we were covered by the security cameras, so it was clear that we acted according to nearly every guideline. I say nearly because I never once said "Freeze, police." No one seemed to have caught on to that fact, or they realized, as I did at the time, that announcing my presence would have done nothing but get me killed. Apparently, the gunmen had already assassinated a few policemen on a lower floor, before we had heard the gunfire. Technically, this didn't affect me or Alex, but realistically, it told the investigators that there would have been no purpose to calling out who we were or that we were on the scene. Unless we wanted to commit suicide, then we could scream out our position as much as we wanted.

Since we were both on an active case, and there was no sign of wrongdoing, we were going to be allowed to keep our weapons and not be benched for the better part of the next week. So we were lucky.

Determining this went on for *hours*. By the time we were allowed to leave, it was already three in the afternoon. If we didn't make it out of the city fast enough, traffic would trap us on the island of Manhattan until dark.

As we walked to the car, Alex gave a deep sigh, and I couldn't blame him. "Over twenty years on the job and I swear I've fired my gun more in the past few months than I have for all the time before that. I stick with you too much longer, I may get a reputation as a gunslinger."

I shrugged. "I wish I could tell you it's going to get any easier. But it's not."

"Ugh. Yeah. I know. I know."

My cell phone rang. I hadn't known that one of the miracles around me also included diving through a hallway full of water and my cell coming out intact. I picked it up, took notes, and hung up.

Alex saw my face. "What now?"

I sighed. "Remember how we said that the Mayor wouldn't come near this investigation?"

"Yeah?"

"He wants us at City Hall. Now."

Chapter 8

YOU CAN'T FIGHT CITY HALL

Thankfully, Bellevue was on the east side of Manhattan, on First Avenue. It was a relatively easy drive down the FDR Drive to get to City Hall—very relative. While Bellevue was practically on the FDR, and the roads make it relatively easy to get to City Hall, the Hall itself sits in a part of Manhattan where the famous grid system of streets starts to completely fall apart. What few people realize is that the further south one goes, the more the streets are laid out in a fashion reminiscent of when it was New Amsterdam. Granted, navigating the streets to City Hall was better than going to and from the Women's Health Corps headquarters, but not by much.

The "Civic Center" and the surrounding area is fairly crowded. There's City Hall, One Police Plaza, the courthouses, the FBI field office, and it was surrounded by Chinatown on one end, Tribeca on another, as well as the East River and the Financial District.

Unlike most modern buildings, City Hall looked nice. The exterior is French. If you've seen Versailles, you see the influences overlap. It was solid stonework through and through. The interior was obviously from an age where architects cared about making things look nice.

There was one major problem the moment I opened the car. The smell hit me again. This time, it wasn't isolated to a person or a room. Evil was everywhere.

I whispered to Packard what I could smell, and he shrugged. "It's politics. Of course it's evil."

Once I got into the building, it only got worse. I couldn't tell if I should get an exorcist for the building or blow it up...with or without occupants. Unlike the abortion headquarters of the WHC, there was no ebb and peak. It was a constant flow of evil. This was one part body farm, and ten parts sulfur. I was worried that if I struck a match, the entire building would explode.

We were met and escorted to the Mayor's office. It looked like any you would have seen on television: dark blue rug, off-white walls, camel couches, a table, and a desk. It was also very linear—it was designed so that everything led to the desk at the head of the room.

Mayor Ricardo Hoynes was, for lack of a better term, a blockhead. I wouldn't have been at all surprised if his skull could fit neatly into a rectangular box. He was mostly gray. His eyes were so brown, I was certain that some prune juice would change his color to blue. Despite his name, he was whiter than I was and kept trying to pass for Hispanic. His claim to fame within the Barrio (Spanish Harlem) was marrying a Miami woman who had backed Castro...and was run out of Miami soon after.

Today, he wore a hideous pink tie with tiny blue stripes, a pale blue shirt, and a gray suit.

"You've had an eventful day, I hear," Hoynes growled. "You've not only managed to piss off the Hispanic community but also everyone of African-American heritage, as well as a major city industry! Is there anyone else you'd like to alienate? Like the Jews? Perhaps you could set Chinatown on fire."

Alex shrugged. "Which one? We have three."

Hoynes pounded the table. He was less than intimidating. "This isn't funny!"

I held up a hand to eye level like a kid who knew the answer in class but didn't want to be called on. In my best Peter Falk impression, I said, "Pardon me, sir, I'm confused. How did we manage to do...any of that? Our day was spent repelling an attack on Bellevue by a notorious criminal gang that spends most of its time preying on other Hispanics. We also asked a few questions at the employer of a murderer in a prior case."

Hoynes stood and leaned over his desk in an attempt to be intimidating. "First of all, the Women's Health Corps is a major provider of women's healthcare in this city."

I raised a brow. "Truly? Last time I checked, 95% of their services were abortions."

"Which prevents a drain on city resources," Hoynes answered. "And removes a high-risk criminal element."

Both brows went up this time—even on Alex. Since over 40% of abortions were black children, I was surprised he was so blatant about a statement that amounted to "the fewer black children born, the fewer criminals." I had to restrain myself from correcting him. It was a common mistake in statistics where the correlation of two sets of numbers was mistaken for causation. *Roe v. Wade* made abortion legal in America, and the crime rate went down several years later. There were some people who concluded that all the children aborted in that stretch of time had been an entire generation of criminals removed before they could be born. For some reason, a lot of pro-"Choice" politicians were happy to use that in their arguments to keep abortion legal. Few people put two and two together that the downturn in crime correlated with the end of the crack wars.

But even if I wanted to correct him, I couldn't get a word in. Hoynes kept ranting. "And MS-13 is a provider of immigration to thousands of poor foreigners whose only crime is that they were born elsewhere."

I tried to keep my face neutral at that bit of stupidity. At the time, I guessed that he referred to illegal immigration—which was an odd way to refer to sex slavery, human trafficking, child prostitution, and the laundry list of MS-13's other violent offenses that involved heavy artillery and RPGs.

Hoynes just couldn't stop talking. He must have loved the sound of his own voice. "And how dare you insult and malign an ancient African religion by linking it to the murder of children."

That's when I blinked. "Excuse me?"

"Moloch is an African deity," Hoynes told me. "Going back to a great, ancient African empire! Looking into Moloch-like this is racist! How dare you. It's religious persecution!"

The depth of the stupidity made my brain freeze, which was probably for the best. I couldn't imagine what response would have allowed me to keep my job.

Alex's response was "Moloch was worshiped with child sacrifice. We can't link it any closer to child murder."

Hoynes rolled his eyes at the ignorant peasants and dismissed the statement with a limp-wristed wave of his hand. "Please. All *rational* geneticists and medical professionals know that we shouldn't allow any rights to children before they're ten years old. Carthage was just an advanced culture, incredibly far ahead of its time."

If my brain were like unto a computer, I immediately settled into a phase that could only be described as "the blue screen of death." It felt like every word out of his mouth was mere gibberish. The Tower of Babel itself couldn't have made him any less incoherent to me. I couldn't tell if this was strange political posturing (after all, we were the only two people in the room, and he had only just finished his first year in office), or if he was really that stupid. Yes, he was left-leaning, and the left in New York City profited off of minorities, illegal immigration, the WHC, and even the criminal class.

But to claim that MS-13 was "just" an organization that shuttled illegals over the border was insane—even the State Department considered putting them on their list of terrorist organizations, and they had to be browbeaten to put Al-Qaeda on the list. And labeling Moloch as "advanced thinking" just made my brain hurt. He threw in the Aztecs on top of it, just for fun, I think.

Who's briefing this idiot? And what drugs are they on?

Hoynes continued for a while, accusing us of being racists, religious bigots, Inquisitors, and whatever other politically correct terms he had in his vocabulary. It was less a matter of us sitting there and taking it and more a matter of us tuning him out, as though we were locked in a room with a screen full of static.

I tuned back in around the time he said, "I know you cops hate me—"

"That would require us to think about you," I shot back.

I stood. I was suddenly angry at the browbeating. I started praying just to keep my temper in check.

"Look, Mister Mayor," I continued. "I don't care. I don't care about you. I don't care about anything you just said. I don't care about your political problems, your political stances, or your strange stump speech. We're doing our *job*! As much as you don't like it, one of the NYPD was nearly murdered last night, along with his family. All we're doing is investigating it as best we can with the paltry clues we've been given. Markings on the perps connect them to a former employer. It doesn't matter to me *what* or *who* that employer is. If the mooks who shot at my family were covered in Russian tattoos, I'd have spent my day down in Brighton Beach talking to the Bratva. And no, I didn't care about the race, creed or ethnicity of who shoots at me. MS-13 had AK-47s in Bellevue, and they were killing anyone who got in their way and some who they used for target practice just because they could. As I told President LaObliger, we will investigate this without fear or favor. There is no fear of her or of you. And you can be damned sure that we want no favors from either of you. Now if you'll excuse us, we have to go back to work."

Hoynes glared at me for a long moment, and I met his eye right back. I don't know if I had merely had my fill of crap that afternoon, or if it was something about Hoynes that did it.

"Next time you want to talk to us, you can talk to our PBA reps."

My cell phone went off. I didn't even break eye contact as I reached and grabbed my cell without looking for it. When it didn't ring again, I quickly checked it. "That's a text from the morgue. If you'll excuse me, we have to drive for the next hour to get out to Long Island. If you don't mind, we have to get back to work."

Hoynes kept screaming at our backs as Alex and I walked out the door. Alex waited until we were down the hall a ways, then said, "Wow, Tommy, I didn't even think you could get that angry."

I frowned, unable to explain what exactly set me off about Hoynes, and so suddenly. I was used to political garbage being dumped on us. I had been a cop for over a decade. I came in during Mayor Bloomberg's first term, and the politics had only made the Job harder over time. I should have been used to it by now. In fact, I thought I had been. "You and me both."

"I like the fake-out with the ME's office. I mean, Nassau? Really?"

"No. Really. Apparently, the local morgue is full right now. But there's plenty of room over in Nassau. Sinead's going to meet us there."

Chapter 9

ON ICE

Technically, it's only about fifteen miles from Manhattan to Nassau County, in the *political* entity of Long Island. The geographic entity of Long Island was just over any Eastern bridge from Manhattan. The political entity starts at the Eastern edge of Queens, not far from my precinct. The first stop in political Long Island is Nassau County.

Nassau County's medical examiner office is unique, due to its proximity to two major airports. If you've ever seen a morgue with a wall of refrigerated drawers, you have the idea. Now make those walls tall enough and long enough to accommodate the bodies from a collision of two jumbo jets.

Doctor Sinead Holland was a pretty brunette with a heart-shaped face. Despite having her career, she had smile lines starting to form. Her background was Northern European, up near Norway, giving her high cheekbones, and eyes that were nearly Asiatic Lapland.

Right now, she was with the collection of men who had tried to kill me early that morning. They had all been sewn up, and looked... even more dead than they had at my house. She was in scrubs and gloves, with a medical mask down, tied around her neck.

Alex and I walked in, and ME Holland gave us both heated looks. "What's the idea?" she barked, furious. "Come on! What's the joke? Are you *trying* to start an investigation? Don't you have *enough* to do without *wasting my time*?"

I held my hands up in a timeout formation. "Could you back up, please?"

She didn't. "Where did you get them? Some other morgue? You guys had me so fooled with the cameras at your house, I believed your story. I swallowed it whole and entire. How did you pull it off? Did you do some sick marionette parade with them? Film it in advance and jigger the timestamp? What?"

"Sinead," I interrupted, "we have no idea what you're talking about. What did you find in the autopsies?"

"I didn't find anything." She shared her anger by glaring at Alex. "I wasn't even able to autopsy them."

I frowned and pointed to the stitches. "Did they come with the needlework then?"

"Yes. They did." She reached over to a table and grabbed a file, then slammed it down in front of me. "They were autopsied over a *week* ago."

Alex and I exchanged a look. We were both thinking the same thing. This was ominous and disturbing. Calling our target a death cult was one thing. If they had power over the dead? That was something else. And after dancing with a demon a few months ago, nothing seemed out of the realm of possibility.

Holland studied our reaction. "You didn't do this?"

I gave her a look. "Of course not, Sinead." I stepped forward, looking over the men who had attacked my family. One had gone down with a bullet in his brain. Apparently, another had been caught in the throat. "I guess I shouldn't ask if this one suffocated."

Holland shook her head. "If he died last night, it wouldn't have been from that. The bullet lodged right in his spinal cord. He would have gone down like a puppet with his strings cut. This, of course, assumes that the first three bullets didn't kill him."

I furrowed my brow, not liking the sound of any of this. I didn't even want to consider what this would mean. But if we had been attacked by the walking dead, then taking out the brain and the spinal column would have done it...at least, according to the usual media on the topic.

"What happened with the original autopsies?" I asked.

Sinead frowned. "Apparently, the ME who carved up the attackers the *first* time ... he died last week."

Alex started. "Really? What happened? Too many formaldehyde fumes? He fell face down in someone's organs?"

Sinead shook her head. "The ME had been killed during an S&M session. The Mistress who killed him had a defense lawyer who argued irresistible impulse, as something 'Just came over her.' Though she couldn't say what the steak knife was doing in the bedroom in the first place..."

I flinched. This looked worse and worse the deeper we dug. I had zombie henchmen, with guns, breaking into my house and trying to kill me. There might be mind control involved, just to cover up evidence. This didn't even count the mayor trying to shut down the investigation and the violent, terrorist-level street gang occasionally remembering that I'm still on their hit list.

While I still had trouble believing that I could become a saint, I had a lot less trouble believing that I would become a martyr.

How much worse could it get?

Remind me again why I'm not in witness protection?

Doctor Holland gave us a look that said, very loudly, that she was waiting patiently for our answers, and she wanted it right now.

Alex shrugged. "Would you believe me if I said zombies?"

Holland looked from Alex to me and back again with a raised eyebrow. Her shoulders sagged, and she sighed. "Maybe it works better for me than the more elaborate plots that would make this work. But even those don't add up. Why would...anyone fake all of this? Sorry, Tommy, but it's been weird ever since Curran."

Alex scoffed, amused. "Sinead, you have no idea."

Holland gave him such a look. "No, *you* don't. I did the post-mortem. Then I had Bert and Ernie in here for days, trying to strongarm me into saying you did something untoward to him."

I blinked, and looked at Alex. He shrugged. I glanced back to Holland. "Who?"

She studied us both for a moment. "Bert and Ernie?" She paused a moment, waiting for us to understand. "The Internal Affairs guys?"

We got it at once. "Oh."

I nodded. "You mean Statler and Waldorf."

Alex laughed as he shook his head. "Seriously. Get your Muppets straight."

I was still amused, but also confused. During everything with the demon, the IA guys had been fair, patient and unbiased. Despite all of the odd crap that had gone down, Statler and Waldorf had kept their heads. What had changed? Had the Rikers Island incident been the last straw for them? Or had my presence alone given them cause for concern? After all, Curran had made it very personal with me. If IA had presumed I took it just as personal and exercised a vendetta against him, then I could see where they were coming from.

Except not even that made sense. Statler and Waldorf had seen on video (and told me themselves) that I had ample cause and opportunity to kill Curran before I arrested him. So what had changed? Either something had changed their perspective, or they thought something had changed mine. Offhand, Rikers had been the turning point. It was the only thing that made sense at the time. From their point of view, perhaps killing Curran on Rikers was the same as killing a perp in custody.

Thankfully, Holland wasn't one who could be pressured into turning in results made to fit what the investigators wanted. That had been a genuine problem in some crime labs.

"Besides," Holland continued, "there's another problem."

I held up a hand. I was suddenly hit with a strong smell of evil. It was almost as bad as the stench around Curran or City Hall. "Everybody, out, now."

It was too late.

The morgue drawers started to rattle and shake. The wall of drawers made a racket akin to a category-five tornado. The metal shelving clattered and banged as though the corpses were desperate to escape their captivity.

Then the drawers began and slide open on their own.

Chapter 10

COLD COMPANY

As I noted earlier, this morgue was designed to accommodate recipients from two jumbo jets colliding and killing everyone aboard. In this case, that meant room for over 1300 bodies.

Which meant a storage facility with drawers thirteen high and a hundred deep.

The drawers on the far ends of the morgue wall slid open first. They popped open from the bottom level up.

And then it was raining bodies.

Some of the dead were half-wrapped in body bags. Some of them came down in parts...but even the parts were moving. Disarticulated hands pulled arms along by the fingertips. Arms pulled along burned torsos that had been severed from the lower bodies. One of them was headless. I didn't even know how it could see where it was going.

More drawers opened, from the far ends. The drawers opened to block off both means of exiting. The drawers kept opening closer and closer to us. I looked up. Thankfully the top rows right above us hadn't opened. Yet.

"Sinead. Get behind us and pray," I said as I drew down and started firing. I aimed for the closest whole body and aimed for the kneecaps. When it dropped the corpse to his hands and shattered knees, I fired again for the shoulders. It ended up thrashing on the floor. It didn't stop when I shot it in the head. But with all of the important joints broken, it couldn't move.

I kept firing as I tried to both pray and cycle through the various and sundry zombie types I knew from fiction...I was just going to ignore scopolamine. As a street drug, that merely made living people susceptible to suggestion... There was the standard virology perspective that made bodies reanimated by something blood-borne—it was the majority of the *Living Dead* movies and *Resident Evil* films. But that mythology at the very least killed those zombies via headshots... There were necromancers, where nothing stopped the zombies except total destruction of the walking corpse or the death of the necromancer... And there was the traditional voodoo, which I knew little about. Mythology about the walking dead aside, I could recall that scientists realized that there was biochemistry involved in making "real world" zombies, where a person could be drugged, important parts of the brain could burn out due to poisons, and then be perfectly amenable to taking orders. But like scopolamine, that required the person still be alive.

As I prayed and meditated on the issue, my vision split, as though I had been playing a video game in first person, and it went from single player to cooperative.

I looked right, and into my own face.

I didn't know how I bilocated, or what triggered it, aside from God giving me what I needed to get out alive. I had heard nothing from Sinead behind me, so I presumed her focus was on the walking dead. Or maybe the falling dead. Then again, Alex didn't make even a grunt of surprise, so the horde of zombies acted as a good distraction.

I dropped to one knee and kept firing...

The duplicate me looked at the top drawer of refrigerated units and knew we would be facing undead from above any minute. So as I continued firing from a kneeling position, I also leaped on an empty slab, then started to climb/fly up the drawers, locking them as fast as I could. Like the last time I had to "levitate" during a battle, I couldn't tell how much was great jumping skills—in this case, almost like parkour, jumping from handle to handle—and how much was actual flight. Either way, it was a mad scramble up, and I locked three columns of drawers on the way up. I jumped/flew over to the next column, and went straight down, throwing the switches on each drawer so I locked everything I could reach...

And then I looked down at the floor. I noted my firing stance. I could appreciate my own aim from a third person perspective. But there was also the sight of the horde. Dozens of zombies had already touched down. But five columns of drawers had already popped open, with thirteen drawers per column.

I had to stop myself from doing that math. I didn't even glance at the forces aligned against Sinead and Alex. I couldn't waste time. But assuming that an equal number of drawers had opened on the other side of the room, they faced a similar number. Meaning there were already over a hundred walking corpses on the floor, trying to kill everyone.

To be fair, I had always found zombies in media to be boring...

But I must admit, facing over a hundred of them with no way out certainly increased their scare factor.

Back on the tiled floor of the morgue, I kept firing, but I had only so many rounds. I had over a hundred rounds on my person, but when most of the bodies took four shots to drop, it ate through my ammunition quickly. At the rate Alex fired, he might be out before I was. We had sounded like the pistol range at the FBI Academy, where one of the things they tested was how fast the candidates could fire pistols as well as shotguns. My first pass was for knees. My second pass was for shoulders. Unfortunately, by the time I was done with the first pass, I needed to reload for the second.

Suddenly, a shotgun blast went off behind me—behind both of me. On the ground, I was too busy reloading my pistol to look for the source. But as I reached the bottom drawers, I spared a glance. Sinead hadn't hidden behind Alex and me. She had grabbed a pump-action shotgun.

This explains why she didn't see me bilocate, I thought.

Alex also looked at Sinead. Alex blinked as he noted me hanging out near the ceiling. His eyes barely flickered from me at the drawers to me at his flank.

Alex looked back to Sinead. "Where'd you get that?" he asked her.

Sinead racked it, looking at Alex, and not me. "We keep a lot of bodies here. Some that are important. The first round was for a warning blast with rock salt." She squinted at the corpse she shot. "Though it worked."

There was only one stone still corpse, not even trying to move.

As I went back to work shutting drawers and shooting zombies, I racked my brain for which zombie type was affected by salt.

Voodoo.

Yes, I know. Earlier, I mentioned that Voodoo "just" used biochemical tricks and biology to create the effect of the zombie. However, in the mythology where they believed they created the walking dead, a little salt went a long way. Apparently, that part wasn't a myth.

Remind me to just assume that dark magic crap exists across the board, and not to dismiss it with "what scientists say really happened." Scientists obviously don't observe half as much as they think they do.

Now, if there's some sort of Voodoo priest working around here, that might explain why the headless bodies and random limbs are still moving. They're not sensing us, the Voodoo priest is using his eyes to guide them to the targets. Which means he's here.

The version of me firing from a kneeling position on the floor refocused from the corpses shambling my way to the doors on the other side of the morgue. I could see a tall shape at the other end, his head level to the security glass. He watched without moving. I had problems imagining that he was frozen in fear.

I aimed for the man in the shadows. He moved before I fired, putting two holes in the glass.

The free-range body parts and the headless bodies suddenly became very unfocused, crashing into other corpses.

"Sinead!" I called over my shoulder. I made certain to call from the floor, so Sinead wouldn't look up and see my levitating duplicate. "You got any more rock salt?"

"In the desk," she answered before she fired again. This time, it was buckshot, and the corpse staggered but kept moving. "You thinking Voodoo?" she asked.

I considered inquiring why she was so quick to accept the super-natural and how she leaped straight to the same source I thought of … but there was no other explanation for the walking dead and the reanimated body parts. As for connecting the effectiveness of the rock salt to Voodoo? Her job was dealing with the dead. If she didn't seek out media around zombies, people who consumed zombie media probably came to her. All it took was one late night watching a rerun of *Kolchak: The Night Stalker* on cable to figure that out.

Alex holstered his pistol, took the shotgun, and started firing. "Get it. I'll empty this." He cycled quickly through five more shots before he was out. His first blast had taken off a head. He, too, noticed the corpses without a head now had problems. He switched back to his pistol when the shotgun ran dry. He passed the shotgun off to Sinead when she came back with the box of shells. As Alex burned through his ammo, she reloaded.

It also helped that all of the drawers I sealed up as I levitated were on their side. The zombies they cut had through weren't getting rein-forcements.

On the other hand, I was down to my final magazines. Three more, and I would be out. And I didn't want to go melee with a horde of zombies. I think that fell under "Test not the Lord thy God."

Against the wall of death, I finally ran out of drawers to lock. Trying to figure out what to do now, I checked my magazines on my levitating body. When I had bilocated, I had duplicated all of the ammunition I had on me at the time. As I locked all of the drawers, I hadn't fired a single round.

Excellent.

I "ran" along the wall, though the levitation made it look more like I took bounding steps on the moon, allowing me to cover the room in a matter of seconds. I landed next to myself...and nearly slipped on the expended brass. I steadied myself and resumed firing with fresh ammunition.

On the other hand, my other body had only one magazine left, and a collection of bodies heading our way. I felt a little useless, having two bodies active and only one able to fight.

I frowned, narrowed my eyes, and looked at the two bullet holes in the door. The Voodoo priest who raised all the zombies might be the way to put them all down.

I stood, gauged the distance, and prayed that this would work—otherwise, I would have to save myself from my own stupidity.

I backed up a few steps and took a running start—not because I lacked faith, but because if God decided to work with me, I wanted to meet Him at least halfway. I sprinted for the line of corpses and leaped before I reached the first one. I went straight up, and over them. I landed behind them and charged for the doors. I kicked it open and moved through, clearing both ways before I burst into the hallway.

The hallway was empty. The security guard at the front desk had been killed, his entire head removed. Symbols had been made in his blood on the walls.

What is it with the demonically inclined and finger-painting in blood? Are they all evil five-year-olds at heart?

A shape caught my eye, and I saw a shadow fleeing down the hall-way. I fired off a round, and it kept moving. I started running to catch up until my feet left the ground. I had gone from running to levitat-ing. Cue the John Williams theme to *Superman*.

I literally flew after the perp. I got him within sight relatively quickly. He was a tall and lanky shadow, swathed in a cloak. It billowed out behind him like a living cloud.

In his hand was a single-edged machete.

You might wonder why I didn't just open fire right there and shoot him in the back. If I was correct, he was assuredly more dangerous than any gunman. For the record, please note that I only do that in the midst of firefights already in progress, when the perps outgun me and when I'm certain that saying "Freeze, police" will only get me killed. I also wanted him alive. He had to have some sort of answers, and I wanted to have a long, in-depth conversation when I caught him.

As I closed with him in the hall, back in the morgue, the zombies dropped. One moment they were active and closing in on the three of us, the next, they fell over in piles of cold meat. I holstered my gun and considered whether or not I should give myself backup out in the hall. But the version of me flying through the hall still had fifteen rounds. I was only after one guy. I was *flying*. Did I really need to back myself up? Not to mention that if I left and the zombies rebooted, that would leave a problem for Alex and Doctor Holland to deal with by themselves.

Out in the hall, I was almost on the Voodoo priest. He whirled, slashing out with the machete in a great silver arc. I came in low, under the swing, going for his leg. I had my hands out, ready for the takedown. My shoulder rammed into his shin, under the knee. My hands cupped behind his Achilles tendon, holding the foot in place so he didn't stagger. The leg had only one way to go: backwards.

I brought him down, but he kicked loose and flipped to his feet with a laugh. It was a deep, musical laugh, like some sort of Geoffrey Holder playing Baron Samedi in an old James Bond film.

I bounced up and away, out of his long reach. Though he was lanky, looks were deceptive. When I grabbed him, I felt muscles like coiled cable. I couldn't do much in the poorly lit hallway. He was all shadows and cloak. He was more a demonic version of the Shadow.

The first swipe was high. I leaned back, out of the way, and kicked out with my right leg. He pivoted his left leg, knee bent, so my kick was blocked by his shin. I recoiled and burst away from the back-handed swing.

My gun came up, and I barked, "Freeze, motherfucker! Hands on your head!"

Yes. There were times I devolved into street patois. It was universally understood, crossing the language barrier. The gun helped.

The shadow only paused a moment. There was a flash of bright white teeth, and that strange, baboon-like laughter. He leaped backward into the dark. I fired low. The bullet sparked against the wall. He should have been there. I should have hit a body part. A hip, a leg, something. I stared into the abyss, and the abyss probably stared back.

There was no way in Hell I would blink.

* * *

MY VISION COLLAPSED into one sight again. I was in the morgue with Alex and Doctor Holland, and not in the hall with the Voodoo priest.

Alex holstered his gun and gestured at the mess of gore and viscera around us. It was one part Jackson Pollack, one part Hammer horror film. "No DD5 has 'zombie attack' on it. I think I would have noticed."

Sinead lowered the muzzle of the shotgun. "Maybe we can file it under Tommy's little trick."

Uh oh. "Huh?" I said, trying to play innocent. *If she caught me being in two places at once—*

"I saw you locking drawers while you were shooting behind me. Cute trick."

I closed my eyes and sighed. *Lord, I've read that SOP is to keep stuff like this between me and my confessor. It would help me keep things on the DL if you didn't put me into this position. Again.*

Chapter 11

COME OVER FOR DRINKS

The fire was intense but brief. The story was spun by Alex and Holland. I was less concerned about telling lies in this case and more worried about my ability to keep a straight face.

There had been over a hundred bodies shot in the skirmish and then set on fire. The story about teens / psychos / cultists / "the usual suspects" breaking in, killing a guard, and setting bodies on fire was preposterous. It was pitched as "a theory," but the cops who responded seemed to buy it. I wasn't going to argue. By some miracle, the bodies were unnecessary in any homicide investigation. They were from wrecks, accidents, smaller fires, a few crashed private planes, a car pile up, and other messes. In short, we were lucky. Or maybe it had been planned that way by the zombie maker. After all, if the bodies used to attack us weren't essential evidence in a homicide, there would be no reason to investigate them if someone smashed up the corpses or the morgue they were in. It played just as well for the man using them as a murder weapon as it did for us.

Perhaps that was paranoia speaking, but this was post-zombie attack. I think I'm allowed.

After the mess was over, Sinead told me, "You owe me a drink. A big one."

I smiled. "Hard to argue with that."

This conversation would need all the help it could get, and just a few drinks seemed unlikely a solution to all of this. This required a full dinner conversation. I needed all the witnesses I could get, so I invited Alex along as well. And since I didn't want to have to explain things I barely had a grasp of, I invited Father Richard Freeman over as well.

Thankfully, we had our table set up at our new home.

The new house was a nice place. It was a little big for three people, but it was close to the station with room to grow, and cheap. The price came because the home's biggest feature was its history. It was the home of the first woman to be executed in the state of New York. This hadn't been a problem for me, since I didn't believe in bad juju, ghosts, or Voodoo. This last part was before I was attacked by zombies, but the payments had already started. We didn't have anywhere else to move.

The major problem was the way the street was laid out. Our house was on the corner. The street in front of our house, 93rd Road, had a stop sign. The street on the side of the house, 222nd Street, had none. The people who parked on 222nd Street parked up to the corner, cutting off sight lines on 93rd Road. This created conditions so dangerous that the house diagonally across the street from us had four-foot tall concrete pillars on the corner of their property to stop another car from hitting their house for a third time. (I asked.)

"Should I even ask?" Alex said, looking at those pillars.

I shrugged. "People come through 222nd like maniacs."

"Not by the station."

"That's because no one speeds by the police station."

Alex frowned. "People really speed through at an angle?"

I shook my head. "No. The cars come in from the east on 93rd Road at high speed, stop at the stop sign, and then barrel through without looking around the parked car at the corner ... where the cars coming north up 222nd Street hit them, also at full speed. That makes the house with the pillars the corner pocket for the automotive eight ball."

Our new dining room was larger than our last one, and I was grateful for it. It was more than long enough for the six of us. I sat at the head of the table. Mariel was on my left, nearest the kitchen. Jeremy was right next to her, trying to be mommy's little helper. Alex was on my right. Father Freeman was at the other end of the table, with Doctor Holland between the two of them. It was less a matter of bracketing her in, and more a matter of having a witness on one end, and the reassuring presence of a priest at the other.

Thankfully, Mariel's plan of attack was cooking enough food at the start of the week to last the three of us for most of the following seven days. She didn't even blink when I called to tell her we'd have double the number of diners. I thought that the worst that could happen was that we'd be ordering pizza—yes, I know, the agony, the suffering, the horror, pizza for dinner. Heh.

But once we were all settled with portions of meatloaf, mashed potatoes, and sauteed broccoli, Holland looked at us dubiously, as though plying her with food was the lead-in to a massive bribe, or perhaps an oath of *omerta*.

"So, when would anyone like to tell me what's going on? I like Tommy as much as the next person, but being two places at once is a little peculiar, even for him."

Everyone chewed thoughtfully. Except for my son. He may have swallowed his food without chewing so he could answer first, and fastest.

"Daddy's a superhero!" he exclaimed enthusiastically. "He stopped the demon from haunting the house, and then, when the demon grabbed me and Mommy, Daddy came in and shot the demon up and arrested him. But the demon cut Mommy, and then Daddy prayed over her and held her throat together until it healed up all on its own, and she bounced right off of the stretcher and scared everyone! Then when the demon tried to take over a jail, Daddy went over there and put them all back in their cells and told the demon to go back to Hell!"

Everyone at the table went deathly silent at so many uncomfortable, odd truths spoken in such a condensed, slightly exaggerated format.

Except for Holland. She laughed a little and smiled at Jeremy. "Doesn't every little boy think his daddy's a superhero?"

Jeremy bounced in his seat a little. "But it's true!"

Holland kept her smile as she looked around the table. It faded as she watched us. "Is it?"

Alex gave her a slow shrug. "Kinda?"

I lowered the knife and fork. Since I couldn't tell what she felt, I thought it best not to explain the insane concept with sharp implements in hand.

"You see, Sinead, I do have some various and sundry..." I looked to Freeman, silently begging him for the right words.

The priest picked up on it. In a gentle voice, he interjected, "Abilities that could be considered supernatural." He gave Jeremy a kind smile. "Or super-heroic."

Jeremy nodded so enthusiastically, I was a little afraid he'd become an adrenaline junkie by the time he was twelve.

Holland's big round eyes traveled from Freeman to me, then to Alex. "And you, too?"

Alex held up his hands defensively. "Hey. I'm not saying anything."

She narrowed her eyes. "Uh. Huh. You are not saying anything very loudly. You should be the first skeptic."

Alex's head and shoulders bobbled back and forth, as though balancing scales. "I can't be. I got a better look at the circus trick of his you caught at the morgue."

Holland looked at me. "You really can be in two places at once?"

I nodded.

Holland looked at Mariel. "And you? He healed you?"

Mariel gave an easy smile as she sipped on her wine. "I think if you're being technical, he was just the carrier."

"And the demon?"

"Oh," Alex said, "that was Curran."

Holland's look was sharp. "The serial killer? I knew he looked evil, but are we serious?"

Alex's face and voice were dead serious. "Yes. We really are."

Freeman nodded and lightly touched her arm. "Remember when we looked over the autopsy reports for Curran's bodies, and we were both a little put off that *Tom* had to tell *us* that the method of death looked like a partial..." He gave a glance at Jeremy and finished it as "medical procedure?"

Holland frowned. "It did seem odd that we didn't catch it. Like Tommy said, it was almost like the killer had the power to...cloud ... men's ... minds." Her eyes narrowed. "No."

"Didn't you find it a little odd that no one asked a lot of questions around Curran?" I asked.

Holland frowned, her brows furrowed. "I told you this morning, your IA stalkers were in my lab after that."

I shook my head. "I don't mean that. It's less about the body and more about what Curran himself did. Has anyone asked how Curran could have hurled a police car through my front window? Flip over another at Creedmoor? Or why chairs were embedded in his ceiling?"

Holland's frown deepened. She looked to Alex. "You saw this?"

He nodded. "Absolutely. Curran hurled the chairs at us with his mind. Hand to God, and I was stone sober at the time."

She fell silent for a long moment, turning her attention to the food in front of her. Two forkfuls went by before she said, "I suppose it makes sense. If the bodies in the morgue can come to life and come after us, a demon shouldn't be out of the realm of possibility. In fact, it should make the zombies at least mildly reasonable in retrospect." Holland's eyes flicked to me. "And you can heal people? And be in two places at once? And climb like Spider-Man? How?"

I frowned, embarrassed. "I'm sort of something that's called a Wonder Worker."

She cocked her head. "A what?"

I sighed and rubbed my eyes. "For lack of a better term, I've been given an overflow of God's graces, and that comes with a certain set of supernatural skills."

Jeremy, in a low voice that attempted to mimic certain film trailers, added, "That makes him a nightmare to creatures like demons."

I shrugged. "Sure. Like that."

Sinead arched a brow. "So, you're a living saint?"

I groaned at the term. "Sure. Why not? Sort of."

There was a long pause as Sinead looked around the table at us. This was probably a worry that outranked demons and Voodoo zombie minions and death cults—what if she didn't believe us and decided to have us all thrown into the deepest, darkest booby hatch she could find? If she reported that we were all mad here, IA would believe her over us (especially given how IA felt about me lately), and the legal battles would be equally insane.

Eventually, Sinead merely nodded. "Yeah, that makes sense."

My jaw dropped a little. I had hoped for acceptance, maybe tolerance, but casual and total agreement? "Makes sense? How?"

"I can see you as a saint."

I blinked, flabbergasted. "Why does everyone keep saying that?"

She gave me a sardonic smile. "Have you met you?"

I didn't growl. "What makes you say that?"

Sinead rolled her eyes. "Name me an activity you do on your free time that isn't church or charity related."

"What does that matter?" I asked, frustrated. "Do you know how many families across American invest time in church-related activities?"

I closed my eyes, said a really quick prayer, and opened them again. "Anyway, one of my abilities is to smell evil." I frowned, thinking it over. "Which is odd. I've smelled evil on Rene Ormeno, on Christopher Curran, and at the morgue. But somehow, not at my house this morning?"

Freeman leaned back in the chair and shrugged. He folded his hands over his stomach and stared up at the ceiling for a bit. "Just a guess? Perhaps there was less evil involved in motivating the three bodies that invaded the house. The people who broke and entered were whole when they walked in...well, they had eyes. Therefore, they didn't need to be guided like a missile, they could find their own way. Therefore, there was less for you to smell. Perhaps at the morgue, there was more of the dark forces involved to animate them. Perhaps you smelled the Bokor."

"The what?"

"A Bokor. Vodou sorcerer."

Alex chuckled. "You mean Voodoo, right?"

Jeremy grinned. "Who do Voodoo?"

Alex sighted down his index finger at my son like a gun. "Don't start with me, kiddo. I saw that Bob Hope movie before your father was born."

Jeremy giggled, and said nothing, just smiling.

Freeman ignored the childish antics from both my child and my partner. "It's pronounced Vodou by the practitioners."

I nodded. "Well, that's nice. But my tolerance for other religions stops when one of them tries to kill me. Now, 'Bokor'?"

Freeman leaned back in his chair. "The Bokor is supposed to be evil or good, but I think we can dispense with that distinction for the moment. They create zombies and charms that are supposed to house spirits within them."

My eyes narrowed. "Spirits? Like demons?"

"Also souls." Freeman thought a moment. "There are a few ways to look at zombies. One is biochemical."

Holland shook her head. "Nope. Not this case. I know what you're talking about. Those poisons cause brain damage, leaving a living person who responds to commands. These zombies were canoes."

Jeremy paused mid-bite, "They were boats?"

Holland spared him a glance. "They had their organs removes, so they were hollow inside."

"Ewww! Gross! That is so *cool*."

Kids. What can I say?

Freeman nodded towards Holland, giving her credit for her answer. "In which case, another method is where the Bokor takes the soul of a person and uses it to animate the corpse, so the person is basically decaying while the soul is still there. There's possession of corpses and just plain reanimating them. So, pick your nightmare."

Holland held up a hand. "Wait a second. Doesn't this *help*? How many Bokors could there be?"

Alex snickered. "Would you like to help us canvass every occult shop, Santaria shop, and Botanica in South Queens, darkest Brooklyn and the Greater New York area?"

Holland fell silent. He was right. It would take forever to ask at each of them, and by the time we were done with the first handful, word would almost certainly spread.

I decided to ignore that part and move along. "And here's the problem with canvasing those shops?" I added. "I don't have much of a description aside from tall and lanky, and a shadow. He might be bald. And he has really white teeth. We can assume he's Black because I don't know of *many* people who practice Voodoo who are Caucasian. Even if we assumed he lived in the Jamaican or Haitian neighborhoods—which, for all we know, he resides out in Montauk —he'd see us coming, and I suspect that would probably get us killed."

Freeman raised his knife as a point of order. "Not to mention that if this Bokor hung out in the neighborhoods filled with those from the Caribbean, he would risk being recognized for what he is. The boogeyman does not move in with people who acknowledge he exists. The Devil prefers to hang out with people who he's already convinced that he *doesn't* exist."

Alex sighed, and sliced off another helping of meatloaf, adding a thick layer of ketchup as frosting. "Better and better."

The rest of the conversation went around and around over the events of the last few months. We kept coming back to the same two suspects repeatedly for the Death Cult. Outside of MS-13 or the Women's Health Corps, we didn't have anyone. Both had overlap with the worship of demons like Moloch or the Aztecs, but that was it. We also kept coming back to the same problem. We had insufficient evidence to drill down on either suspect.

What if the cult had nothing to do with either group? What if the demon had been allowed to choose its own host? It would then have no direct connection to Curran other than the supernatural force inside of him.

The conversation went through dessert and continued after Jeremy conked out early.

Just after he left for bed at 8:00PM, the doorbell rang.

I answered it, less because I wanted to be a gentleman and let my wife sit, and more because I wanted to make certain that if our unexpected caller was going to do us harm (again), I could meet him or her with the necessary force.

What I didn't expect was Assistant District Attorney William Carlton. He was big enough to block the view of the street from the open door. He looked like he should have played on the defensive line in his youth, and a waistline nearly as wide as his shoulders. His salt-and-pepper beard had passed needing a trim a few days ago. His blue shirt and black tie were just neat enough to avoid being referred to as "rumpled." He was swathed in a great black coat and topped with a wide-brimmed slouched hat. His cane was a long black piece of wood with stainless steel at both ends. He looked like some variation on a GK Chesterton cosplayer.

"Hello, Detective Nolan. I hope I have not caught you at a bad time?" He spoke at a measured pace, in a deep resonating voice, but his words spilled out in a sharp, clipped manner.

I shook my head. "We're actually finished with dinner. I have some friends over."

"Ah. Work friends or civilians?"

"Work. Would you care to come in?"

"Please. I'm here on our mutual business."

I walked him into the living room and introduced everyone. He took up a position in an overstuffed armchair. He declined my taking his hat and coat. He leaned forward on the chair, hands atop the silver head of the cane, hat dangling from one hand.

"To begin with, I had heard early this morning about all of the various and sundry bizarre occurrences that happened to you last night. I was also informed about the shootout at Bellevue. I must give you my condolences on once again being dragged into circumstances so above and beyond the normal purview of your average police detective. You can be assured that I have been brought up to speed on the official reports about both incidents. I inquired with your Lieutenant before I left the office, and he explained the reasoning behind your investigative track. Is there anything that I have missed that hasn't been part of any official reports? For example, like your abilities as a wonder-worker?"

Everyone's jaw dropped. Carlton looked puzzled as he glanced casually around the room. "Did I say something wrong?"

Mariel recovered first. "How did you figure it out?"

He gave a tight-lipped smile. I could tell because the bush on his face moved. "My dear Mrs. Nolan, I was one of the privileged few who had access to the security footage of Rikers Island. While other people had believed themselves savvy enough to conclude that your husband's appearance in three places at once was merely the result of the time stamp on the footage being corrupted during the riot, I looked over the reports. I studied rates of speed, and who among the prisoners reported certain events. I constructed my own timeline of the situation and knew that the only way Detective Nolan could have done what he did was to have been in no fewer than three places at once. When I realized he possessed the power of TRI-location, I investigated the phenomenon. The only people who have ever had this ability have been saints who were wonder-workers, and—supposedly—demoniacs. Having met your husband, I easily decided that the former was the case and not the latter. As I had already concluded that Christopher Curran had been a victim of possession, it was not out of the realm of reason that a wonder-worker was an option. After all, if the powers of Hell were unleashed upon the Earth, it was certainly logical that the converse was also on the prowl.

"Now, if you please," he continued, "could I be updated on the various and sundry aspects of your case that the department has not been privy to thus far?"

* * *

WE DID, and we left nothing out. Mariel and I explained the attack this morning. Alex broke down the Bellevue assault, starting with our conversation in the padded cell with Rene Ormeno. Doctor Holland detailed the morgue deluge. Father Freeman added the occasional line of commentary.

Carlton nodded sagely by the time we were done. When we finished with the hamster wheel reasoning we were trapped in, he again looked bemused. "I do hate to state the obvious, but I had just assumed from the outset that LaObliger and the WHC had set the forces of darkness against you, as retribution for destroying their pawn and the demons within him. After all, he worked for them. I never believed that no one, at all, could have completely and totally missed an evil that could allow a demon inside them.

"As for legal cause in the real world—especially if you need political cover—you can link one of their employees to symbols found in the attempt on your life. That's the first connection. Second, if you take LaBitch *at her word*, Christopher Curran interacted with *no one* outside of work. Therefore, the only suspects you have are all tied into the Women's Health Corps, as they are the only individuals who have any ties to Curran. Hence, currently, you have no one else to investigate.

"From *our* point of view, with the knowledge that *we* possess, you know, and I know that Curran was infested with a demon. More *importantly*, he was possessed by a demon that was deliberately guided by the people we're looking for. Which means that Curran wasn't picked out of a hat by this cult. Someone knew him. Indeed, I would conjecture that the cult picked Curran because they already knew he was a monster."

Again, the rest of the room was silent. I had not interacted with ADA Carlton since the Rikers Island incident, so I had forgotten that he spoke in whole paragraphs.

Alex was the first to react. He grimaced. "Why didn't we think of that?"

Carlton straightened. "You did. It was the exact logic that you had originally used to discuss the case with your CO. You were perfectly correct at the time. You only failed to realize that it was cause to keep digging into the WHC. You disregarded the original premise once you had used it to fulfill your original intent. In fact, had I been your commanding officer, I would have told you to focus *all* of your attention on the WHC. Tear their world apart. Root out their rot. And burn whatever was left."

I arched my brow. I wasn't used to hearing such things from anyone above my rank. They were usually too interested in being politic. "I gather you don't like them much?"

"I dislike LaObliger," Carlton answered. "Her style of politics is vile, and she herself is monstrous. You were in my office when she was there. That was not an aberration on her part. That is who she is.

"There is also one bit of data in my possession that you may not be aware of. It is generally kept secret from the public. You have mentioned that Moloch was originally worshiped by having children thrown into a fire pit. The Women's Health Corps has currently increased their shipments of 'medical waste' to an incinerator to generate electricity. Not only is he worshiped by fire once again, but he is also providing them with a profit at the same time."

I nodded. He had a point. "In which case, we need to go after them with both barrels. But that leaves us with only one question. LaObliger gave us Curran. Why would she do that if she was holding his leash?"

"Depends on the ultimate plan. Perhaps Curran was meant to end in prison. Perhaps LaObliger isn't in on it, but members of her organization are. You won't know until the digging starts."

Chapter 12

INTO THE DEPTHS

I sat on the edge of my bed and started to pray. I honestly didn't want to go door to door in every abortion clinic that Christopher Curran had worked at. The list was at a dozen different clinics spread out across the Greater New York area. It was a bit of a nightmare. At the low end, it would take an hour at each of them. I don't even think I made it through a whole sixty minutes at the WHC main branch in my two visits there combined.

I sat there with my face in my hands, focusing on prayer. I was going to need all of the fortifications I could get in the morning: a breakfast of daily communion. Catholics eating Christ's body, blood and divinity was my baseline... This was more like Agony in the Garden time.

"What's the matter, Tom?"

I started, coming back to the world around me. Mariel was already dressed for bed and under the covers with the lights out. I still had my work clothes on.

I explained my trials with the Women's Health Corps facilities in the city, the smell, and how it basically pounded me down. I slipped into bed, and she wrapped her arms around me immediately.

We fell asleep as we whispered prayers together.

* * *

Alex Packard picked me up from the church on our way to our tour of abortion mills that Christopher Curran worked at.

You can imagine that it was just as bad as I thought it was going to be. If you took the Kermit Gosnell case—where an abortionist had basically committed every crime against medicine, God, nature, and the laws of Pennsylvania—broke it up and spread it throughout the WHC system, you had an idea. Trying to find nurses was impossible. I couldn't find a licensed employee for love or money in one place. One place that proclaimed to be "a clinic" had a stack of vaccines stacked in a corner, outside of a refrigerator. I'm not a doctor, but I knew that was a problem and a half.

Our trip had started at six in the morning. We had managed to get through the two abortion mills in the Bronx, followed by two more in Manhattan, by noon. The visits were all relatively quick. My reputation had preceded me. As you can imagine, the answers to many of our questions involved either "Never heard of Christopher Curran" or "Talk to my lawyer." We showed them photos of the men who had tried to kill me the other night. We asked them about anyone with an unusual interest in anthropology, Aztecs, ancient Carthage, history, politics, or having a pulse.

The last two didn't even get a reaction.

The two things that ate up most of our time were the traffic and our stops to church after every clinic. Fifteen minutes in Christ's bodily presence, and I was good to go again.

The "clinic" in the Bronx actually pissed me off. It was more like a butcher shop, only not as clean. There was blood on the floor. Alex told me the air smelled like urine, though I couldn't smell it over the stench of evil. I actually found a flea-infested cat in the hallway—I grabbed a broom and pushed it out the door. Alex and I had to watch our step because the cat had used the stairs as a litter box. The women who were there for appointments seemed like they were already drugged before the procedure began, or still drugged out of their minds afterwards. They were on dirty recliners covered with blood-stained blankets. We passed the operating room, and I think it could only have been cleaned if I set the room on fire, then sprayed it down with a few gallons of Lysol. The instruments in the OR were stained with blood or rusty.

At this "clinic," tiny body parts were seemingly stored at random throughout the clinic—bags, milk jugs, juice cartons, and cat-food containers (maybe the cat did belong to someone). Jars with baby feet lined the shelves of someone's office. We went down to the basement to talk to the janitor, and there was various and sundry medical waste piled high.

After that one, Alex joined me at the nearest church. He took longer to recover than I did.

The entire experience was soul-deadening. Neither one of us could even consider lunch. We both settled for a bottle of water and some tasteless protein bars and only because we had enough problems feeling ill without adding a lack of food on top of that. We both spent time researching having an abortion clinic shut down for health code violations. It is nearly impossible.

Two boroughs down and a venue change later, our next stop was just south of my house, south of Jamaica Avenue. This was in the operating area of "gangster" Daniel David DiLeo (call him 3D at risk of your health). D was a work acquaintance. Despite his features being summed up by "big Black guy," that was the only stereotype around him. He and his crew were largely crooks who saw crime as a business. It was how they made their money. They were borderline respectable. They dressed in black, with leather jackets, but their black shirts were professional, button-down collars with the top button undone. There were a few scattered black jeans, and they wore their pants belted around their waists.

They were, pardon the expression, white-collar criminals.

I sent D a text that we would be in the area, and that I'd want to talk with him after I was done at the abortion mill in the area. He sent me a text asking me if I wanted him to burn the place down. I was a little taken aback by the offer. He had a little smiley in the text—possibly for the plausible deniability later on to say he was joking—

but arson was usually out of his wheelhouse. Then again, he did have a little girl with a girlfriend, so he was conservative as far as criminals went. But so was *The Godfather*. I simply replied with a quick "No thanks," and didn't look for a follow-up. I would inquire with him later to see if there was a deeper meaning to that, or if he was a very specific definition of "pro-life."

Alex drove us to the Jamaica clinic. This one was a little cleaner, though we walked into the middle of havoc. It was noisy, and not in a "normal office day" noisy.

We entered the lobby right behind a couple. A man dragged his girlfriend behind him. She hit him with her free hand, while he held the other. They screamed at each other in Spanish. He had made an appointment for her in the clinic. She didn't want one.

He wound up to punch her when I stepped directly into his eye line. I moved back part of my coat, showing off the badge on my belt.

"Is there a problem?" I asked in Spanish.

He was taken aback, surprised by our presence. The girl broke away and bolted. He stood staring for a long moment. I recognized the look. He had had experience with the cops before and probably more than just a passing acquaintance with traffic cops. There were even tattooed teardrops by his left eye, usually a prison tattoo.

"No problem, officer," he said in English. His eyes focused on the door, where the girl fled and sprinted for the door.

He tripped over Alex's foot. The delay cost the former inmate enough time that the girl caught the bus before it could pull away from the stop. He cursed at the bus, eating its dust.

It was the only good feeling I had as we turned back to the abortion mill we had to walk into. I was starting to presume that Curran only worked in the lowest of the low. Probably because he enjoyed it.

Before we got to the main desk, there were two screams at once. Both were on the other side of the front desk, in two different hallways. "I'll go right."

"I got left," Alex said.

I went right because that was where I had heard the baby cry. It came from behind a door with a pane of security glass in it. The room was a simple table. There was a premature baby on a tray. The man above him wore an apron and held a set of scissors, moving close towards the baby's neck.

That's when I kicked the door in, gun drawn. "Freeze. Police. Back away from the baby and drop the scissors."

He looked at me, confused. "What? We do this every day." He looked back to the baby and hadn't moved away at all.

The term there is "failure to comply with a police officer." That's when I took two steps forward and slammed the heel of my foot into his hip, essentially collapsing his body. He crumpled to the floor like paper. I stomped on his wrist to get the scissors out of his hand then kicked them away. I tossed him my handcuffs. "Cuff yourself to the radiator pipes."

He blinked, confused. "What are you doing, man?"

I racked the Glock. It wasn't necessary and even ejected a bullet, but it got the point across.

"Okay, okay. I'm doing it." He lackadaisically cuffed himself. I holstered the gun, grabbed a sealed package of paper towels (because I *knew* those were clean) and used them as makeshift towels to wrap up the baby, who was still covered in blood.

I heard shouts, only this time they were from Alex.

I frowned, held the baby under one arm, against my side. I drew my gun and raced out of the closet.

Two large orderlies dragged Alex ou into the hallway. One was trying to get his gun away from him.

I raised mine and said, "Freeze, police. Back away from the gun."

The orderly stopped struggling with Alex for a moment, kept one hand on Alex's wrist and used the other to flip me off. He then grabbed for the gun again.

Without any hesitation or remorse, I shot him in the face.

The other orderly backed up so fast, it wasn't even funny. His hands went straight up, and he threw himself against the wall.

I held the gun on him and nodded. "Good move. Alex?" I called over the baby's cries.

"A girl changed her mind about getting an abortion. They're not letting her."

Alex charged into the room. Sure enough, there was a teenage girl being strapped to the table by two other orderlies. We came in, guns up. I circled around them so my back was to the wall opposite the door. I didn't want the orderly in the hall to change his mind.

I smiled at the orderlies, though I was so angry, I was almost certain I bared teeth at them.

"Hi, everybody. Let the girl up, or I kill you both."

No, I wasn't kidding. This was not an empty threat on my part. I had no patience anymore. If I had possessed any to start with, the previous six hours of abortion clinics had whittled it down to nothing. When one man had no compunction about killing a baby, and the other felt no fear about grabbing a cop's gun while being held at gunpoint, I could only conclude that the people here were fearless in the face of the law. Or stupid. Perhaps both.

Right now, the two I currently had at gunpoint were guilty of kidnapping, unlawful restraint, and attempted assault with a deadly weapon, an unlawful attempt to force an unwanted medical procedure against the will of the patient. If we were in another state, I would have added attempted murder to the charge, but the death of a child in the womb didn't count as murder in New York State, only in Federal law.

The girl was unstrapped in a matter of minutes. She thanked us profusely. Her rapid-fire Spanish even confused me, and I was proficient. But it didn't matter. I learned everything I needed to when I heard only two words: *Mara Salvatrucha.*

She was one of MS-13's sex slaves.

Meaning that this abortion clinic was where MS-13 came to "fix" their "problems" when their sex slaves got pregnant. And we were in the middle of it.

"We have to get out of here," I told Alex. "We have to get *everyone* out. Right now."

Then the gunshots started.

Alex and I dropped to a crouch. The girl rolled off the table and landed on her hands and knees before lowering herself flat. The orderlies ran out of the room, and straight into gunfire. They forgot the first rule of making a deal with the Devil—the Devil has a right to reneg whenever he likes.

Alex moved for the door. I moved for the girl. I handed her the baby and said, "*Keep her safe. We'll lock you in.*"

I went next to Alex. "What is it?"

"At least two guys," Alex said, quickly peeking out the door. "Both with automatic weapons. Hispanic, I think."

I quickly considered what happened. My first thought went to the tattooed man we encountered on the way in. He didn't have the full facial tattoos of Rene Ormeno, but he could have been with MS-13. If this is where they went to get their sex slaves "fixed," then why not?

What were the odds that Christopher Curran had worked in an abortion mill that serviced MS-13?

"Just our luck," I muttered. I tapped Alex on the shoulder. He backed up. I moved to the door frame and peeked around the corner. I couldn't see anyone. I darted across the hall to the next door over.

I fired the moment someone popped his head out. He was covered in tattoos, MS-13 style. I missed, and he fell back. I fired three more times, even though he wasn't there. I wanted him to stay back or stay down, either way.

The door behind us banged open. Two shots went off, instead of fully automatic fire. Alex had my back, and I didn't even need to look away to check.

Right now, this was a standoff. MS-13 wanted me dead, and they'd have to work to get to me. If they were smart, they'd know they'd have only a few minutes before the cops showed up. Depending on the traffic, it could be anything from five to fifteen minutes. We might be able to hold out for five minutes. In fifteen, we'd be dead.

"Five! Four! Three! Two! One!" they screamed from the office.

That can't be good. I ducked back, as did Alex.

The bullet storm started. I nearly hit my head on the fire extinguisher. I didn't even think about it but grabbed the extinguisher and hurled it out into the hail of lead. The extinguisher exploded, releasing an entire fog of retardant to fill the hall. I fired into the office then back into the open door behind. Alex picked up the idea, and we both fired in calm, measured bursts. We didn't have another bullet storm. They didn't know where we fired from, but they couldn't advance while we were shooting at random.

It was bad enough that I carried 200 hundred rounds of ammunition every day. If I survived this, I'd have to have a talk with ESU about carrying artillery. We had a shotgun in the car, and it wasn't doing us any good.

Bullets kept coming in full automatic fire. They were shooting blind. At least, the stalemate was still in place.

I ejected the magazine and reached for a fresh one. The second the magazine hit the floor; a man burst from the floor, crashing into me. He had crawled along the floor and through the fog. It was smart. He bear-hugged me, pressing my weapon against the wall and out of my hand. I elbowed him in the temple. His hand was pinning one wrist. So I pounded the back of his hand to break the grip, making one hand pop open. With my other hand, I grabbed some fingers and bent backwards, peeling his hand off of me. I jammed my fingers into his eyes and the palm into his nose. His head went back, exposing his neck. I released the hand and hammered the side of his neck, going for the vagus nerve. He crumpled. He still had his machine gun. Apparently, he hadn't wanted to shoot me when he was out in the open in the hall.

Unfortunately, the fog of fire retardant had dissipated. But now I had a machine gun. Ho. Ho. Ho.

I flipped the gun to semi-automatic. I couldn't fire blind the whole way, especially not into the office. Again, I wasn't going to use a gun I never saw before for target shooting.

Then the grenade rolled down the hallway.

Chapter 13

D EX MACHINA

Alex and I hit the deck about the same time. The grenade went off, breaking the windows, tearing holes in the cheap walls, and blasting the doors off the hinges.

Between the shooting, the fighting, and the explosion, my head was ringing. I was largely deaf, and I couldn't focus enough to make certain that I could hit between the door frame.

I rolled over on my back, gun up, and hoped that I could hold it up long enough to dissuade the gunmen from coming in. Heck, given the state my head was in, I was hoping that I could aim through the dust and the smoke from the explosion.

The ringing in my ears stayed with me, muffling everything, even the sound of automatic fire. There were no bullet strikes. I heard no return fire from Alex. *What's happening out there?*

As my hearing cleared after a minute or two, the automatic fire was still going. Only this time, it was coming from outside.

Did the cops arrive and bring SWAT?

More shots came from inside this time. They were gone in seconds.

After a moment of silence, two hands slowly came into view in the door frame, as though someone were holding their hands up. They were big and black, and I recognized some of the rings.

I lowered my gun and called out, "D?"

The gang leader stepped into view. His black leather jacket and dress pants were immaculate. Despite all of the dust in the air, he was untouched. He gave me a big grin, then reached down, offering me his hand. I took it, and he hauled me off the floor.

"How you doing, man?" he asked casually. I had to read his lips since my hearing was still on the fritz.

"You'll have to speak up a little," I answered. "But when my hearing comes back. I should be fine." I looked down at my body. There were no holes or perforations. "Where did you come from?"

He shrugged. "Me and mine were down the street, checking out a local establishment that we had considered purchasing."

I frowned, thinking that over. Then I realized that Alex wasn't joining us. "Packard."

D moved out of the way so I could come through. I went straight to the other office as I stepped over the bodies in the hallway. Alex was on the floor, his body covering the girl's. In turn, the girl's body was almost wrapped around the baby.

I stepped over and tapped Alex on the shoulder. He started, and his gun stopped halfway to me. "Oh. Hi."

I gave him a little finger wave. I didn't see any holes in him, and it was going to be awkward enough with one of us half deaf. I turned back to D and noted that no one else was with him. "Where are the others?"

D grinned. "Others? What others? I just showed up, Detective. Why would you think I had anything to do with how these pitiful miscreants met their end?"

I blinked, taken aback. If that's how he wanted to play it, I wasn't going to argue with him. "Took them out with your bare hands, did you?"

D laughed. "Of course." He looked up and down the hallway. "How did they even find you?"

"I think we tripped over an MS-13 spotter in the lobby. He was dragging a girl behind him."

D rolled his eyes. "Probably one of their trafficked girls. Yay." He patted me on the shoulder. "You're lucky it happened in my area of operation. We disapprove of gunplay unless we start it."

"No argument." I shook my head, still amazed. "How lucky could we have been? We arrived, and within a minute, saved a baby from being murdered, a girl from being forcibly operated on, and were picked out by an MS-13 spotter, but you guys just happened to be a block away?"

"God is on your side, Detective."

I laughed. If he only knew.

D left. He didn't wait to be thanked and didn't even wait for the police to show up and see that he had been there. He strolled out over all of the bodies like nothing had happened.

Then the police showed up. *There goes the rest of our day.* I figured that the rest of the afternoon, and into the evening, would be eaten up by the after-action report. This was starting to look like the investigation into the Death Cult that was after me was going to lead to more property damage than just putting me in witness protection.

CSU, IAD, and ESU all showed up within the next 30 minutes. The Crime Scene guys came to pick apart the shootout. Internal Affairs showed up because it was an officer-involved shooting. Emergency Services came just in case some MS-13 reinforcements arrived late to the party with more guns.

The IAB guys were not Horowitz and McNally, but more local. That made sense, since the only times they showed up in my life was for a high-profile disaster—a shootout and suicide in a police station, a shooting in an officer's home, and for a massive prison riot. A shooting in a neighborhood as low-rent as this end of southern Jamaica was less so. I would have thought that a shooting at an abortion mill would have been headline news—it was, but our dispatch only broadcast the address, not the business. Apparently, even reporters who had police scanners didn't bother to Google the addresses broadcast over the air.

News trucks had not arrived on the scene, but that was more due to the construction of the streets and the neighborhood than anything else. Going back over a hundred yards in this neck of the woods meant that people had to detour around the crime scene about two hundred yards further back than *that*. The news people would be stuck in traffic for hours. It might make the six o'clock local news if they were lucky.

When asked about what happened, I had left out D from my answers. I don't know why, except that I didn't think it would be a good idea. When I was asked if I knew who could have been the third party who intervened and saved our lives, I said "I'm certain that it was another street gang, probably one that didn't like MS-13 on their turf. But since I didn't see any of the shooters, I couldn't say who for certain."

This was true—I didn't even see D with a gun so he may have actually hung back with his men while they did the shooting. None of the investigators asked me if I had any specific gang suspects in mind, certain or not, so I didn't volunteer.

After every investigator on scene had finished talking to us, we were held at the scene for no reason given to us. I was going to argue with the next person who came into the room. It was bad enough that we'd had two shootouts in two days. Even Alex said, "One more, and we get a set of steak knives." But I had been interrogated in the abortion mill, in a back room. Alex felt ill due to the medical waste. The stench of evil was so heavy in the air, I couldn't even smell that much.

When I wasn't being interrogated, I was in a constant state of prayer. I had only had this ability for a few months, and I wasn't sure I'd ever get used to it. But this had been the longest amount of time I had been locked in with the smell of evil without a break. Unlike sifting through a garbage dump for hours, I was fast getting the idea that it was impossible to get to the smell of evil. The moment I had asked about taking the interrogations outside, it had started to rain—thunder, lightning, and a full downpour.

"Just your luck," Alex had muttered.

After twenty minutes of solid waiting—a uniformed guard at the door to make certain that we hadn't been comparing stories—the door opened again.

In walked Mayor Richard Hoynes, along with a bearded gray hair with a briefcase. The gray hair's suit was more expensive than my house, so I immediately pegged him as a lawyer.

"You didn't listen," Hoynes started. In a move so fast I was taken by surprise, he kicked my chair back, with me in it. I hadn't expected him to be that strong. "I told you dummies to stay away from persecuting a religious minority and keep away from the Women's Health Corps." He waved around at the back room. "And here you are, in a WHC clinic, asking about Moloch worshipers. LaObliger called my office to complain about your constant, endless harassment of these law-abiding citizens."

"Indeed," the lawyer added, "His Honor brought this to the attention of the American Civil Liberties Union, and we were simply shocked at the persecution of a religious minority and its right to worship as they deem fit."

Hoynes nodded firmly. "There's nothing to justify this. Nothing. At all. What have you accomplished? First, you slaughter a bunch of undocumented workers at Bellevue, somehow generated a massive mess at the morgue, harassed dozens of innocent medical experts going about their business, interfered in the rightful operation of medical facilities all over the city, all in order to persecute a minority religion in order to satisfy your own personal religious dogma."

The lawyer nodded. "Exactly. This is harassment at the purest level. You obviously don't care about reasonable justification for your actions."

I sat there and barely listened. I had been in a state of prayerful meditation the entire time I had been locked in the back room between interrogators and nothing had changed. I almost thought that the smell of evil had gotten worse, but that was probably just a matter of prolonged contact. I had tuned out Hoynes and his rantings and didn't care about the lawyer.

Alex, however, narrowed his eyes. Apparently, he was even more annoyed with Hoynes now than I was earlier. "Looky here, doofus.

Bellevue was an attempted breakout of a gang leader with delusions of being a terrorist. I have no idea what you heard about the morgue, but that wasn't us. As far as innocent medical businesses, I'm not a health inspector, but I can sure as Hell tell you that the only way to get some of those places clean is to burn them to the ground. This 'rightful medical facility' tried to murder" his arm swung up and pointed out to the hall, presumably at the girl with the child we saved "that baby, and tried to forcibly operate on that girl. How you even consider calling a death cult a minority religion is beyond me. Jews are a minority, you don't see them doing human sacrifice."

"Circumcision is just as brutal, a medieval practice," the mouth-piece interjected. "His Honor concurs."

Alex looked to the lawyer. "You're in New York now, Ha-vuhd, it's pronounced Hizzonor. Second, shut it."

The lawyer sneered. "You still have no cause for doing this."

Alex scoffed. "Tell it to ADA Carlton. He told us we had more than enough probable cause to investigate any and all places that Christopher Curran had worked, and we're doing just that. The Moloch angle is because the demon was tattooed on the chest of one of the guys who tried to kill him!" Alex pointed at me this time.

The Mayor laughed. "Enough. I'll throw you both in jail. I don't care why or what for. Then the WHC will sue you into bankruptcy over that bit of slander."

Alex gave the mayor a look only reserved for the lowest street junkie trying to mug him with a broken bottle. "Too late."

Mayor Hoynes blinked, a deer in the headlights. He hadn't expected the pushback to keep coming. I was surprised that he didn't know something was up when Alex started in on him. "What?"

"Given our experience with the Women's Health Corps, I wore a body camera today. I sent copies of *all* of the footage from *all* of our visits today to friends of mine."

Hoynes sneered. "Friends? Yeah? Where? The health inspector? He answers to me."

"To HHS in DC. And to several friends of mine in the media, particularly Fox News, several radio stations, and a few bloggers I know." Alex jerked his thumb at me. "As well as all of the Catholic news services I've ever seen him subscribe to. And I think he gets all of them." His phone buzzed. I didn't see his other hand, so for all I know, he had triggered the notification himself before he pulled it out. "Oh, look, here's the footage going live on the Internet at...Life Site News...CNS...and Instapundit, and a PJ Media article written by Tom Knighton."

The ACLU douche stepped forward. "That is a misappropriation of public resources."

Alex barked a laugh. "Go ahead, sue me. Try it. Then we can ask why the ACLU all of a sudden has a problem with the police body camera footage that's supposed to be for public consumption when it, you know, *goes public*." He flickered to Hoynes. "Then people can wonder why you're backing dangerously unsanitary abortion mills in minority communities. It's almost like you don't care for the health and hygiene of blacks and Latinos. That'll go over well. How many of them voted for you?"

Alex stood, grabbed my shoulder, and pulled me up as well. He had apparently decided we were done. "Now, unless you have any real issues, we'll be going about our business. We still have one more abortion mill to look at today, out in Nassau so the Women's Health *corpse* can complain about us to Nassau County."

Alex shouldered past them, and I followed. We pushed through the rainstorm, made it to our car, and got out. Alex drove since I was still trying to hold it together. It's difficult to explain just how utterly oppressive the sensation had been. If I didn't know better, I would have sworn that events had conspired to keep me in the abortion mill to have just that effect on me.

We were on the Long Island Expressway to the biggest abortion mill in Nassau when Alex said, "How you doing?"

"I'll live." Even I was surprised at how strained my voice was.

"Doesn't sound like it."

"I'll be okay. I promise."

Alex said nothing for a long moment as he navigated the traffic and the rain. "If you say so. I'm holding you to that."

We still stopped off at a church for a few minutes before the next abortion mill. When I went into the pew, I immediately knelt. I was certain that Alex needed the cool dark of the Church. I noticed Alex kept his eye fixed on the candle next to the tabernacle like some eastern adept using the flame to clear and focus his mind. I shrugged and let him do that as I just fell into supporting arms of the God and his Son and asked for the support of his Spirit.

The building we ended up at was actually a surprise. It was upscale, perfectly modern, and indistinguishable from the rest of the medical buildings surrounding it. Each building had their own suites of medical specialty practices. It was impressive. When we got to the abortion clinic, we couldn't tell by sight. The carpets were clean, the walls were pristine white, the clientele were alert aware and well-dressed. It was almost reassuring.

However, I could tell what it was by smell.

Alex did all of the talking this time. I felt ill. I must have also looked ill as well. One of the doctors came up to me and offered me a large bottle of water. I thanked him and drank half of it down in a few seconds. I thanked him again, and we went on our usual routine. Did anyone know Curran? Who had heard of Moloch? Aztec deities? Did anyone have a healthy interest in Carthaginian or Latin American religion? Anthropology? History? Did anyone know anything? Had they ever heard of Thomas Nolan? Do you recognize any of these dead men? Had they ever *heard* of Christopher Curran? Did they know who was president or what year it was?

The last two questions Alex threw in just to see if they could say anything other than the word "No."

I took a quick break to the washroom after twenty minutes. For some reason, my guts didn't like me and rejected everything in my system. After a ten minute sojourn in their impressively neat bathroom, I was washing my hands when Alex kicked the door in.

"You've been poisoned!"

Chapter 14

POISONING THE WELL

I looked at Alex like he was crazy. "What do you mean I'm poisoned? I feel fine. Okay, as fine as I've been at any of the other abortion mills we've been in. Why?"

Alex raised the bottle of water. "I tried to take a sip. This is formaldehyde."

I blinked. My eyes then narrowed. The pieces clicked together quickly. "Son of a bitch."

I stormed out of the bathroom and looked down the hall. I spotted the doctor who handed me the bottle of water coming out of an office, and he saw me. He met my eye, and he didn't like what he saw.

He ran.

"Freeze!" I bellowed. "Police!"

I was ready to take off after him, but he literally tripped over his own two feet and crashed to the carpet. By the time he had scrambled to his feet, I had him by the collar of his lab coat, hauled him up, and slammed him against the wall. I patted him down, cuffed him, and dragged him out into the lobby.

I read his name tag. "Doctor Borgia? Really? You kidding me?"

I began loudly reading him his rights in front of everyone. By the time I had gotten to "Do you understand these rights as I have read them to you?" the waiting room had emptied out. Alex closed the door behind them and used the lock on the hinge to keep people out.

I shoved Borgia into a chair, hands behind his back. I turned to the rest of the office, and announced in my Sergeant's voice, "Attention! Everyone in this office is officially under arrest. None of you—I repeat, none of you—will be going anywhere until we get the truth out of you."

One of the girls at the front desk sneered. "On what charge?"

I pointed to Doctor Borgia.

"This man handed me that bottle," I said, pointing to Alex, who held up the bottle by the cap. "His hands were ungloved at the time. We have his fingerprints on the bottle. The bottle contains formaldehyde, and nothing but formaldehyde."

I eyed all of them in turn. "That he felt that he could poison me like this means that he had been told by the other clinics we visited today that I couldn't smell anything at the clinics. He rightly assumed that I had been unable to smell the poison.

"In case you weren't paying attention, that he was in communication with other clinics about a method that could be used to kill me and get away with it, means conspiracy. Now, either I get some answers, or we're going to have to assume that each and every one of you is involved in a conspiracy to murder a police officer. In the State of New York, those come with special circumstances. Does anyone know what's so special about them?

"What's special is that New York State, that bastion of left-wing progressive goodness, will happily strap your ass to a chair and light you up like a Christmas tree!"

Everyone in the office bore a passing resemblance to a deer facing the headlights of an oncoming sixteen-wheeler.

"And now!" I bellowed. "We're going to start this conversation *again*! Only *this* time, you people are going to give us straight answers, and you will not jerk us around. Or *everyone* gets to go to jail. And I will make certain that the person who screws around with us will be locked into the cell with everyone else."

I pulled out my phone and called up the photos of the two dead men. I held it up for everyone to see. "I ask you all again—does *anyone* here recognize *either* of the men in this photo? And yes, they are dead. They're the *first* people who tried to kill me this week."

I think phrasing it like that got their attention.

The man in cuffs behind me made some noise. I turned to Borgia while Alex kept one eye on the rest of the room. "Yes?"

He looked uncomfortable, but I wasn't that concerned with his comfort. "Well, yes. Sometimes, trucks come and take away the body parts to go to the incinerator. You know about the incinerator?"

My eyes narrowed. This was about the "medical waste" resulting from an abortion being burned for electricity. "And?"

"Sometimes, they don't go to the incinerator."

Alex stepped forward and nudged his shoulder. "To start with, how do you know?"

"Because the real truck comes afterward," Borgia said nervously. "And it's always different guys with all of the right paperwork. It's scary." He looked at the pictures still on my phone. "Those guys only came by a week or two ago."

"Oh *really*?" I gave Alex a look.

He knew what I meant. Tracing those trucks would actually mean progress. *I'll take any progress.* I looked back to the office. "Can anyone else confirm this?"

Now that they had universally decided not to stonewall us, we were getting more information than we knew what to do with. But the story was the same. There was a weekly pickup for the incinerator. A truck came, took the body parts away, and that was it. But every so often, a "fake" truck would show up. This truck would have *all* the right paperwork. It was indistinguishable from the usual trucks. The only reason anyone knew that the truck was a fake was that the electricity producing plants that incinerate the body parts called to complain that they never showed up, or the real truck did show up, asking for body parts that had already moved on. The trucks were on a rotational roster, so no driver had ever driven up to the loading dock twice.

It was a perfect system, especially if you wanted to slip in a fake truck every so often.

The last fake drivers had been the ones who came to my house to kill me.

"Was there ever an investigation?" I asked.

"No," Borgia whimpered. "The Women's Health Corps dissuades us from calling in the police. We're told that it would all be handled in-house."

I raised a brow at the statement. I had taken the incident against me personally. I guess I shouldn't have.

"What do you mean they frown upon calling the police?"

He shrugged. "It was a company-wide memo. They're worried about some sort of evangelical fundamentalists and rosary praying Catholics coming here and causing trouble at the slightest sign of an issue."

Alex smacked him upside the head. "You mean like my partner here? Is that why you tried to kill him?"

Borgia squirmed in his chair. "The memo on Detective Nolan was simple. You were to be handled. The tone of the message was clear. Will no one rid me of this meddlesome cop?"

I cocked my head to one side. "A company-wide memo?" I looked to the main office. "Did anyone else get that memo?"

A smattering of hands went up. I asked to see it.

There is currently an NYPD Detective Thomas Nolan who is currently trying to shut us down. He is a Catholic and a murderer. He is responsible for the framing and subsequent murder of our coworker Christopher Curran. Every health center he has visited today has already been shut down, pending the outcome of an in-depth investigation that we are certain that he has rigged in advance. He is a clear and present danger to the company. If anyone could handle Detective Nolan in such a way that would keep him out of our hair, that employee would get an automatic doubling in salary. Despite being a bloodhound, he has no sense of smell, so no real sense of taste, which explains his fashion.

·   ·   ·

IT WAS UNSIGNED. It was from a general account.

"Gotta give them this," Alex said, "They sure knew how to word it so that they couldn't be brought up on charges. They could easily argue that they just wanted someone here to impress you so much that you'd go away. And the lack of smell could read like a straightforward insult."

"Hell," Borgia bitched, "how did you even survive? You drank half the bottle."

Alex shot back, "He barfed it up in the bathroom. And you're lucky he did. Now sit down and shut up unless we ask you a question, dumbass."

There are days I'm glad I have Alex to lie for me. There are only so many ways to explain myself without sounding like I'm from a mental ward.

My eyes didn't come off of the computer screen with the memo. "You people don't own the building," I said aloud. "You just rent a suite of offices here."

Alex looked at me, confused. "Yeah? So?"

I looked at him. "How many security cameras did you see outside?"

Alex smiled. "A whole heck of a lot. We only need one from the loading dock—"

"And we can hopefully trace that SOB through traffic cameras."

"Thank God for New York being so desperate for cash they put those cameras practically everywhere."

I nodded and straightened. I grabbed Borgia and hauled him to his feet. "You're still under arrest. We can hold you for a while without charging you. If you jerk us around, file a complaint to be released early, you go from our station's holding cells to arraignment, and I promise you that you won't be in isolation. I doubt you'll get bail for the attempted murder of a police officer."

I looked back to the office. "If anyone here sends a report back to the WHC HQ, I'm coming back here, and I'm going to leave with more of you heading to jail. Am I understood?"

They nodded. I gave them a curt nod in return, and we marched our quarry out the door, into the hall, and pushed him into the elevator. He opened his mouth, and Alex jammed his finger into the tip of Borgia's nose.

"The right to remain silent. Pretend you have it."

The good doctor remained quiet on the way to our automobile. I tossed Borgia in the back of the car, and I smiled, feeling better than I had all day.

Alex looked at me over the car. He checked the windows to make sure they were closed. "So, Tommy. How *did* you survive?"

I shrugged. "When I discovered I had abilities, I looked it up to see what else I could theoretically do." I opened the door, slipped into the driver's side, started the car and put it in gear. I looked at Alex and decided on how to answer his question without tipping the prisoner. "Fun fact: did you know some saints drank poison and survived?"

Alex rolled his eyes. "Drive the car."

Chapter 15

PIECE AND QUIET

The first thing we did after throwing Doctor Borgia (honestly, that name!) in the holding cells was to talk with TARU, the Technical Assistance Response Unit. A lot of what they did was computer forensics. Though in this case, they were the first people we wanted to talk with about tracing the fake van. We had to get around the little hiccup that it was a crime in Nassau, but Alex had to convince them it had to deal with the attempted murder of a police officer. We both avoided using my name. TARU was based in One Police Plaza, and while I trust the Police Commissioner (to a point), 1PP was in the same area of buildings as City Hall, which was at least one borough too close to the Mayor for my taste. Our major hope was that tracking a theft *from* the "Women's Health Corps" was enough to allay suspicions.

There was one unspoken question hanging between me and Alex. Why steal the body parts of aborted babies? The reason it was unspoken was that neither one of us wanted to speak the answer aloud. Somewhere, where the fake truck eventually stopped and delivered its ghastly cargo, there was almost certainly a fire pit and a statue to Moloch.

Nothing more could be done until TARU got back to us. I didn't want to imagine the man-hours involved hunting down the truck. Police procedural technology works better on TV than in real life. Facial recognition is for the CIA or someone with enough computing power to run it. As is license plate recognition software. Or anything else DARPA has created. Unless we were in Las Vegas, where the casinos had money to burn.

So, Alex and I called it a day. Yes, this would be odd for a murder inquiry. Normally, we'd work twenty-four to forty-eight hours straight. But it wasn't yet a murder. I was still alive. On the bright side, as long as they kept trying to kill me, we would still have leads to work. The not-so-bright side was that the people shooting at me only had to get it right once. They would continue to shoot at me until I solved the case, or they got lucky.

At that moment, I was largely frustrated with my sense of smell for evil. When the smell hit, I couldn't tell where it came from. If a lone man was locked in a room, or just showed up, that was easy. If there were peaks and lows, sure, I could sniff them out based on the strength of smell. But the Women's Health Corps installations drove me mad. Was it the people? Just the operation as an act of evil? The institutionalization of abortion? All of the above? Elements like that were the biggest drawback. City Hall had the same problem. I could have shaken hands with Curran in that building and not known it was an encounter with a demon.

Unfortunately, I didn't think that any saint had tried to use sniffing out evil as a detective tool. The only patron saint of cops was Michael the Archangel, and he obviously never wrote anything down like Juan de la Cruz, or St. Therese, or, heck, even any Pope in the twentieth century. After John XXIII, you'd think a memoir or book was part of the Holy Office.

I walked home from the station. I was grateful that we moved only five blocks away. Before I crossed 222nd Street, I waited at the corner across from my house. I studied the short concrete pillars installed at the edge of our neighbor's property line. The pillars had yet to be struck by a car. Which just proved that Murphy's Law was right under the Nicene Creed.

I arrive home at six, a rarity. Mariel kissed me hello, took one look at my face, and sent me immediately to bed for "just a minute," since I "looked like Hell." I'm sure that Alex would have added that she didn't know the half of it. But I wasn't up to taking his place with the snark.

Jeremy ran down to meet me. He stopped when he saw my face. "Dad, you should sleep."

Ouch.

So I followed my son's advice. As I crashed on the bed upstairs, it occurred to me that that moment would have been the perfect time for someone to come and assassinate me.

I was asleep before I could act on that thought.

I woke up with a start an hour later. There was no crash, no sign of alarm, nothing. *I worried for nothing.*

Tonight's dinner was roast chicken, probably enough for a week.

I made my way downstairs, still groggy. I wondered briefly why I was so out of it, but I had started this case sleep deprived, and I'd kept busy ever since. Heck, all of the driving alone would have normally been a drain. Then there was Bellevue, the morgue, the clinic tour, the clinic shootout, were just the frosting on the cake. Why was I surprised to be tired?

I walked to the dining room, and to my surprise, Monsignor Richard Freeman was already seated at the table, a double scotch in hand. "Hey, Monsignor, what're you doing here?"

Freeman smiled and nodded at me. "I thought I would stop by and see how you were. I knew your agenda today would be tough on you."

I made my way to the table and had a seat. "The agenda wasn't the problem as much as everything else. Yesterday also caught up to me. Not to mention..." I leaned over to call straight into the kitchen. "Mariel, did you hear the news today?"

"Nothing local," she called back. "I was mostly listening to national news today. Why?"

"Just so you're not surprised, I had another one of *those* days at work."

I explained to all three of them (Jeremy dashed in as he heard my call to Mariel) about the shootout in South Jamaica. I mentioned everything except what the abortion clinic did. I was not going to have that conversation with Jeremy. Yet.

Mariel came in with a Corningware of sauteed broccoli. "You know, I don't remember you getting into nearly this much excitement when you didn't have these abilities. I'm not complaining, but you may want to pace yourself."

Jeremy shook his head as he drank down a glass of milk. He swallowed in a gulp that made me worried, but he was merely in a hurry to speak. "Nu-huh, Mommy. Superpowers come with trouble. He's now a trouble magnet. Just read any Spider-Man."

Freeman smiled. "Not out of line. To whom much is given, much is expected. You do have most of the practical abilities."

I shrugged with a sigh. "Some days I'd like to be quiet. You realize I've only just finished the paperwork and all the follow-up from Rikers this week. Heck, Statler and Waldorf both gave me the final interview within hours of the Glen Oaks attack yesterday." I gave him a half smile. "I'm not complaining about the workload, but a day would have been nice, you know?"

Freeman smiled. "Blame the forces of darkness."

"Trust me, I do."

Mariel brought out a platter of chicken. She retreated to the kitchen, then came back with the shotgun.

I blinked. "Really? At the table?"

Jeremy nodded, enthused, and couldn't wait to answer. "Yeah, isn't it cool? Mommy wants to be ready to shoot zombies in the *face!*"

"Father, will you say grace?" I said, moving along.

The monsignor bowed his head, then made the sign of the cross over the food, saying "Ruba dub dub, thanks for the grub, yea God!" while Jeremy chortled and attempted to look pious.

Mariel shrugged as she sat by me, shotgun between us. "Your morgue adventure made me think it was a good idea to be prepared. Some rock salt and slugs, alternately. I wanted to be ready for either.

Slugs first, since humans are usually more likely to be a problem than zombies."

Jeremy beamed and bounced in his chair. "Maybe not this week!"

I shrugged. "Can't argue with that."

Mariel nodded. "It's why yesterday was rifle day. Then there were zombies. Today is shotgun day."

Freeman laughed. "How many guns do you have in the house?"

"Eight," Mariel answered. "Rifles for each of us, the shotgun, handguns for each of us and Tommy's sidearm... a few months ago, it was only five. After dealing with Curran and MS-13, we figured that Jeremy needed a handgun, and we wanted to start him with a rifle first. And since both Tommy and I were going to take him, I got a rifle for myself as well."

"After days like this, I'm glad," I said.

Freeman cocked his head. "Should I even ask what your day was like?"

I shrugged. "Manhattan and Bronx traffic for six hours. Gosnell times five on the clinic tour, the shootout in South Jamaica, an attempted kidnapping—two, really—and an attempted murder. Then I discovered a new ability. Drinking poison without ill effect."

The adults looked shocked.

Jeremy just said, "Cool."

I nodded. "So, it's been a day."

Jeremy grinned broadly. "But what's a Gosnell?"

After a long pause from us, Mariel said, "A real-life horror story."

His face fell. "You mean like *the news*? They're *boring*. They'd make Loki's invasion sound like *bleh*."

Mariel smiled. Mission accomplished.

We managed to dance around the topic of abortion like that throughout the meal. We wouldn't go near it, otherwise. But Freeman and Mariel got the gist. I was sure that after Jeremy went to bed, the conversation would become more detailed.

After a while, we switched back to guns. Freeman looked at the shotgun and asked about it.

"Pump action," Mariel answered. "For the capacity and for the sound. The sound is about as good as firing off a shot."

"The sound is just *cool*," Jeremy crowed.

Mariel smiled. "That, too. Do you shoot, Monsignor?"

Freeman took a sip. "Not in a while."

"Come to the Saint Greg's parish shooting club. We go out to Hempstead and use their range."

He shrugged. "I could probably hit the broad side of a barn if I shot from the inside and I could avoid shooting myself in the foot. But I wouldn't want to bet my life on it."

"Let's hope you don't have to," I said with a frown.

Mariel touched my hand. "What's wrong?"

I shook it off. "Sorry. I just have a bad feeling about, well, something that occurred to me before I fell asleep earlier. That this would be a great time to try again to get us. Or me, I suppose. Either, really. Though I can't imagine that an attack at home would limit their goal to just killing me. I don't mean to worry, but—"

Freeman rose, pulled out a book from his back pocket, and said, "Have you had this home blessed yet?"

I shook my head. "Not yet."

"It's time, then, I think."

Before I could accept, I was hit with the sudden smell of evil. In my own house. I reached for my gun as a voice came from the living room.

"Too late," it said in a deep musical voice.

Four men came into view. One of them was bald, long and lanky with bright white teeth.

It was the man from the morgue, what Freeman had called a Bokor. He was dressed in an elegant gray suit with a silk tie with little crosshairs on it.

This is gonna suck.

Chapter 16

HOME IS WHERE THE GUNS ARE

Mariel came up with the shotgun, as Jeremy rolled backwards in his chair, tumbling all the way into the kitchen—from plan 5-A, assault during dinner. Most "A" plans involve Jeremy rolling out of the way. Before Mariel fired, one of the others stepped in front of the Bokor and took the hit for him. He tottered a little. Mariel racked the shotgun and hit him. This time, he went down.

She had said the shotguns were filled with slugs first, then salt. We were fighting zombies all right.

The Bokor, however, leaped back gracefully as a dance move, landing behind another minion.

I drew down and fired for that zombie's head, knowing that if I missed, I'd strike the Bokor. Luckily, all three rounds hit the zombie full in the face, causing it to drop.

Mariel racked the shotgun twice, firing the next salt shot into zombie number three.

Before zombie number two fell, the Bokor was already on the move, flying (metaphorically) for the front door. I chased after him, worried about his endgame. Three zombies did nothing last time.

But why only bring three zombies when there were large cemeteries full of the dead to use?

The Bokor threw the door open and leapt out into the street. I was right behind him.

I skidded to a stop.

The Bokor had disappeared, and the main street, 222nd, was filled with the dead. Some of them even had guns. Others had swords and machetes.

My gun came up of its own accord, and my first thought was, *God, we're going to need some help here.*

Without any warning, a six-wheeled truck barreled through the intersection, running over all the zombies. The truck took a block to stop, and it idled for a moment before starting to back up.

I cautiously made my way to the corner. The driver put on his hazard lights and met me.

"Hi." He looked at the street, especially the weapons scattered all over. "I really hope that these were bad guys."

I looked around. None of the zombies in the street seemed to survive. A few limbs were moving—mostly fingers, a few toes. I kicked the weapons away, just in case...and because a machete in the middle of the street would play havoc with tires. The paving was bad enough as it was.

I patted the driver on the shoulder. "Don't worry. They were." We introduced ourselves, then invited him back in for coffee.

I walked back inside with the truck driver. Mariel was on the porch with the shotgun, waiting. The shotgun had a little sticker of "Nuns with Guns" aiming rifles outside. It was one of the stickers they sold at the church gun club. It was a group from the parish that Mariel had formed after dealing with the Hellspawn of last year. I couldn't remember if it was before or after the soup kitchen.

Mariel asked, "It's all over? That was fast."

"Baron Samedi got away," I joked. "But his army of darkness— more like a squad, really—are gone." I patted the truck driver on the shoulder. "Ben here dealt with them."

She beamed at him. "Would you like something to eat, Ben? We were having dinner when this started." She waved Ben in with the shotgun.

Ben shrugged. He wasn't put off by the shotgun. "No thanks, I'm good. Just ate before I got on the road. Coffee's good, though. Nice gun, by the way. Mossberg?"

She nodded. "Of course. I'll get you that coffee."

Ben sat at the end of the table. Jeremy was already back at the table, cleaning his plate. Kids are odd.

Much of the conversation was about introductions. If Ben was put off by the priest, the cop, the wife, and the kid at the dining room table with the guns, he didn't show it. Then again, he did just run down a horde of armed "criminals" in the street without a blink.

"May I ask, Ben, if this wasn't your first time in combat?" Freeman asked. He'd picked up on it, too.

"Two tours. Fallujah. Will that do?"

Thankfully, the investigation was short. The weapons in the street and the guys in my house was proof that I hadn't gone out to kill people. Ben was clean, so he made a great witness. He ran through 222nd Street at 40 MPH on a regular basis on his way to several shops up on Braddock Avenue. Though this was the first time he'd been in a traffic incident. Since we had never met before, it was clear with Internal Affairs in short order. The CSU was happy to come to a different home of mine for a change. The guys at my last incident knew my house well enough that they helped themselves to make their own coffee from scratch and had easily found the coffee, spoons, filter paper, sugar, cream, and mugs. This latest incident at least gave them a new place to pick apart.

We were done with dinner before the interrogation started. It helped to have a priest on the witness list, especially since it seemed that certain aspects of IA were out to get me, if Holland's description of Statler and Waldorf was anything to go by.

But to be honest, if it were any other cop, I'd be looking at me funny. My home had been shot up four times in the last few months. Add in my on-the-job incidents, there were guys in New York SWAT who had gotten into fewer gunfights than I have. I guess I shouldn't have been surprised to have someone from IA looking at me funny.

Of course, within a few minutes after the first wave, Alex showed up. He looked around, shrugged and said, "Must be a day that ends in Y."

I sighed, giving him a look. "Hey. I'm not that bad. It was quiet for months before all this started up again. Not my fault."

Alex laughed. "Maybe. You get anything off of these guys? ID? More tats? Affiliations?"

I gave him half of a shrug. "Tats, yes. ID, no. I took pictures and sent them to TARU, just to see if they can add anything."

He shrugged. "When in doubt, give work to a busy man. He'll rush just to get it off of his plate."

I nodded. "After a fashion. I'm having TARU do the faces. I'm hopeful that the fingerprints will get back sometime before Hell freezes over. Though I'm not going to hold my breath. We're still waiting on some of the deep dives on the guys who tried to get me yesterday."

"Hey, but you have to give them this. You have been leaving a lot of bodies around."

I gave him a look. I did not need to be ribbed at that moment. I frowned, looking at my phone, where I had taken the pictures. "You know what? It just occurred to me. We may have someone who could identify these guys. We have him in the cells."

Alex's brows rose. "Yeah. You're right."

I shrugged. "It happens."

Jeremy charged us, arms open wide. I swept him up in a hug. "Daddy, are you going to get the bad guys?"

I gave him a squeeze. "We are. We just need to talk to someone at the office."

Alex scoffed. "Yeah. The basement office."

I tucked Jeremy in bed while Alex negotiated my release from the crime scene. I had expected to be at home until everyone wrapped up and turned in, and I would be going to bed. It would have been too easy for this to turn into a lead. But who knew? I expect what I should have done was text it to the desk sergeant and have him handle it, but we were so close, we might as well do it ourselves.

And people wonder why I lived so close to the precinct.

As I left Jeremy's room, Mariel waited for me. She had put the shotgun away, much to the relief of the cops on the scene. My first thought had been that they'd regret it if another horde came back and tried again. We were at the point where Mariel had spent more time at the range than half of the cops in my precinct.

"What happens now?" she asked.

I shrugged. "Not entirely certain, but we may have a lead. The man we apprehended today for poisoning me is in our cells. I'm hoping he can ID one of the men who broke into the house."

Mariel gave a little smile. "I didn't think he'd be trying to ID the blood smears in the street."

"Heh. This is true. We'll need DNA to figure out who most of them were."

Mariel looked around before dropping her voice to a whisper. "Are you sure they were zombies out there?"

I shrugged. There was no other real reaction to give her. "Unless they were MS-13, it seems as though everyone who has tried to kill us was already dead when they started."

She frowned and hugged me tightly. I returned the hug. "Hey, what's that for?"

"I don't want you to die. Last time was so close."

I couldn't argue. I squeezed a little more. "Between God on my side and Alex at my back, I think I'm good. Heck, last time it was a demon. These people are just ... people. Zombies haven't been that effective."

She arched a brow at me. "Yet."

I chuckled. "Now you're just thinking like Alex."

"And where do you think Alex gets it from? Being around you."

"Nah. He came that way."

Chapter 17

KINGS OF DEATH

W e stopped at Doctor Borgia's cell, which was the same one that Hayes (the first possessed by the demon) had hanged himself in. During our walk to the cell, I had a brief sense of dread, half-expecting to find him hanging from the light fixtures.

He wasn't.

Alex gave Borgia a little wave. "Hey there, killer, how are you enjoying the accommodations?"

Borgia didn't say anything. He just sat in his cell, arms crossed, like a toddler throwing a fit by holding his breath.

Alex lifted my phone with the pictures. "Okay, fine, you can talk to us about these people, or we can throw you straight to Rikers. Take your pick."

Borgia growled and came to his feet, walking over to the bars. His eyes widened.

"You got one of them!" he crowed. "Great."

Alex held up his hand. "One of who?"

Borgia pointed at the phone in Alex's hand. "One of the fake truck drivers."

I smiled. I didn't even have to say anything. It was probably divine inspiration, but somehow, I thought I had a solution to our problem of identifying the bodies we had.

I rushed up a flight of stairs to the main office and went to the nearest computer. It took some time with our glacial internet connection, but I finally managed to get to the goal: LinkedIn.

Alex came up a few minutes later, saw me at work, and promptly ignored me. He went on to call TARU and a few other people, trying to crack the whip on IDs. After he was done threatening and cajoling various and sundry people, Alex opened a book.

It took me an hour of sifting through profiles and different keywords.

"Got them," I whispered harshly.

Alex looked up from some book about the attack on Rome by the UN. "Got what?"

"All of them," I answered.

It had been easy, but mostly by working backwards from the presumption that everyone involved led back to the Women's Health Corps. And it answered all of our questions. The men who had invaded my home the first night this week had been volunteers for the WHC, which is why nothing came up in their employment history.

The three dead bodies currently in my home, being processed by the Crime Scene Unit? They were full employees.

It was official. Everything and everyone led back to the WHC.

We had them.

Now, what did we do with them? This wasn't all that much better than having suspicions. There was no one left to interrogate. And unless I wanted to try arresting every member of the WHC for conspiracy charges under RICO (which is so unlikely that I have problems expressing it in terms that made mathematical sense), we were still, technically, nowhere. It would help with the eventual case, once we arrested somebody. It would be additional nails, circumstantial evidence. But we were getting closer. I knew that much. It didn't help that so many of the suspects were dead...before they committed some of the crimes.

It also helped that both the volunteers and the employees who tried to kill me had all worked at the primary headquarters in Manhattan. They rubbed elbows with President LaObliger every single day.

Note to self: interrogate her in the morning. Perhaps in ADA Carlton's office. I suspect he doesn't care what the Mayor says. Also, he'll probably love what I have on the mayor.

Carlton...

I pulled out my cell phone and dialed. At the same time, I turned the monitor to Alex so he could look over the profiles of all of our dead. On the second ring, I heard, "You have reached the office of ADA William Carlton."

I waited for the beep. When it didn't come after a second, I said, "Hello?"

"Yes. Detective Nolan?" Carlton asked.

I looked at my watch. It was already after ten o'clock. "I'm surprised you're in this late. What's up?"

The ADA grunted. "That's most days. My wife says she likes the quiet. What can I do for you this fine evening?"

I didn't even know how to react to his comment, so I skipped to his question. "You can tell me how you found my house yesterday."

There was a long pause. "I put it into GPS. You're not easy to find."

I groaned. *Some people...* "I mean the address. How did you get my address?"

"Oh. That," he said absently. "I called your station house and asked. They knew who I was and where I was calling from. Why do you ask?"

Aw crap. "How many people do you think could do that with a cop's personal address?"

Yes, I knew that was a list before I asked. I hoped that a political power player like Carlton would be able to narrow it down a little.

Carlton sighed. "Anybody above your Lieutenant, sadly. You could ask around your station, but I wouldn't wish to place a bet about your ability to find the one who gave out the invitation. Unless you come with a lie detector?"

I winced. I was barely comfortable with the people who I was obligated to tell about my condition. That Carlton had deduced it deeply disconcerted me. That he referred to it as though it were an option in the toolbox of my skill sets was a little too casual. "I don't. Sorry."

"At least not yet," he answered. "It isn't a problem. You're the one who will have to worry about it. How goes the case?"

I sighed but filled him in on everything we knew thus far, since last night. He was pleased that we had someone to leverage Doctor Borgia (to which he said, "Seriously? How dreary and unimaginative.") and that we had more ties to the WHC ("It will help the case at the end of the day").

I also warned him about the Mayor. At that, Carlton became quiet, which was odd in a man who spoke in full paragraphs.

When he finally spoke, he said, "You will need something with which to cover yourself."

I smiled and told him that I did have something up my sleeve.

The ADA laughed evilly. "Good. You may just survive this particular idiocy after all. I had not considered that you were capable of such sagacity and advanced planning. Then again, the Bible says to be as innocent as doves and as wise as serpents, so I suppose that you're just being a good Catholic."

"In both cases, I hadn't even thought about it," I said.

"Heh. Maybe you were briefly possessed," he joked.

I opened my mouth but paused. It occurred to me that one of the many prayers of my youth (okay, and even a little more recently) had been for God to just take me over and have me act the way He would want me too. I had deliberately framed it as an open invite. So maybe I had been possessed.

Or maybe I just have good instincts that kicked in while I was traumatized by the endless evil clogging my senses and assaulting my brain. Try not to accuse God of breaking His own rules of free will, would you?

"Anyway, most of our day is going to be spent tracking the van, I think," I told Carlton.

Carlton paused for a moment, humming a tune only he knew. "At least, you have an explanation for why all of those body parts were so strangely preserved at all of those abortion mills the other day. It seems your Moloch cult is company wide—or at least can send company-wide memos that no one has contradicted or perhaps detected."

"Maybe."

There was more humming. I guessed that it meant that he thought so hard he couldn't talk and think at the same time. "Perhaps I can make things easier on you through a certain presumption. Because much like your particular flash of inspiration earlier, I find myself in much the same position. Where did you say that the good doctor was from?"

"Nassau County." I gave him the address. "Why do you ask?"

"I ask because I found myself looking up the contact information on a certain someone the other day. Please hold while I type something into Google Maps. I need some directions, and I suspect that GPS would use the same route, as everything seems to run on Google operating systems lately. Give me a moment."

I did, humming the theme to final *Jeopardy!* as I waited. I had started my second repetition of the theme when Carlton came back on the phone. "Now, I am going to give you a path for TARU to look at. Because it is West on Marcus Avenue, then North on Lakeville Road, then East on the LIE service road, North on Community Drive, and then they make a right into King's Point. Do you understand?"

I wrote it all down. When I read it back to him, he said, "I will wait for your phone call."

I hung up. Alex pointed at the screen. "You want to explain how you did this?"

I shrugged. "Keywords on LinkedIn. Women's Health Corps, employee or volunteer work. That was it. And it's all public domain."

Alex frowned thoughtfully. "Sometimes, they just give it away. Aren't you glad they're stupid?"

I smiled and leaned back in the chair. "All the time."

He pointed at my phone. "What was the call about?"

"I wanted to see how ADA Carlton got my home address. Apparently, anyone above the rank of Lieutenant could get it, and I suspect any politician who gives enough money to the Women's Health Corps can get it, too."

Alex didn't need it explained to him. "Well, I wondered how they found your new address so quickly. Good call."

I frowned. I wouldn't have called it "good." I picked up the phone and dialed our contact at TARU in charge of tracking the truck from the Nassau abortion clinic where Borgia worked. I gave them the route the Carlton gave me, and they told me to hold on. It was apparently a simple matter of plugging in the directions as they went, and scanning a few minutes of film on fast forward.

When TARU came back on, the first words were, "How did you know?"

I blinked. It threw me. "Um...I'm not sure. I guess I just...got a tip from a friend. Thank you. What exactly did you find?"

"We saw them going into King's Point," our friend from TARU began, "but there aren't any street cameras in the area. There isn't any Lojack on the truck, obviously. You're probably going to have to get the locals to tell you something."

I didn't say anything but thanks. I also told them about the LinkedIn solution with identifying the bodies. TARU wasn't happy about it since they had already invested over five man-hours into the problem, but they were glad to not have to pull all-nighters on everything.

I hung up with them and called Carlton back. "You were right."

Carlton didn't seem surprised. "How far into King's Point did you trace it?"

"At the entrance to the neighborhood. Apparently, they're very concerned about who goes in and out of the area, but they don't care about who speeds while they're inside."

"They wouldn't be," Carlton answered. "Please consider that this is old money. I live in an expensive area in Great Neck. But King's Point is another tax bracket and a few more zeroes. Good luck canvassing them to see exactly where the truck stopped. And getting a warrant. And..." Carlton drifted off with a sigh. "Will you be awake in a half an hour? I might as well head home. Your home is on the way. I can make it quickly at this time of night."

"Huh. Okay. Before you hang up—how did you know to look for King's Point?"

"Oh? Didn't I mention? That's where Joanna LaObliger lives."

Chapter 18

NOW WHAT?

ADA Carlton made it to my house around the same time that Alex and I did. The investigators had left. Everyone seems to have accepted that this time had been a break-in, even though we hadn't installed the cameras yet. Although several people left confused about how one of the men had died just from being shot by rock salt. The conclusion was "Just leave it to the ME." Someone had suggested that Holland had been interested in strange dead people so she would get the benefit of the bodies.

I didn't even snicker.

Carlton's familiar slouch hat and cane emerged from his car as I approached the corner. "ADA Carlton."

He smiled. "Saint Nolan."

I cringed.

The ADA laughed. "You really don't like that, do you?"

I shrugged. "It's bad enough that I do enough good works publicly that everybody around me hears 'I have the ability of saints,' and they don't bat an eye. I take Jesus' instructions to go pray in a closet very seriously."

Carlton looked me up and down. "Only if you have a walk-in closet. How tall are you?"

"Six foot ... something." I shrugged.

I never really considered how tall I was. I was big. I've fought bigger.

The bush on the ADA's face moved. There was a smile under there. "Indeed. Come along, we have much to discuss. Where is your partner?"

"He's bringing the car. He doesn't want to walk down, then walk back just for the car so he can drive home."

He nodded. "Good idea. Come, we must discuss this."

I walked in. Mariel and Freeman were seated at the dining room table. Mariel had brought the shotgun back out, and a box of shells sat at her side. We usually had a policy of no guns *on* the table, but in this case, it only made sense.

"Since we had the church gun club meet today, I thought I'd get a fresh box of shells," she told me.

I nodded and blinked. I caught a whiff of evil, which surprised me a little, but then, I had been able to follow the scent at a crime scene once, so that shouldn't have surprised me too much that something lingered.

Mariel looked at Carlton and said, "Hi. Nice to see you again. What are you doing here?"

He swept the hat off of his head and gave a little bow, his bulk supported by the cane. "I've come to have a conversation about exactly how we need to deal with this current problem."

Freeman leaned back in the chair, hands over his stomach, waiting to hear the latest. "Yes?"

Carlton picked the armchair again, and he angled it towards the dining room to include Mariel and Freeman in the conversation. "You see, since the beginning, I thought it was the Women's Health Corps. You probably gathered that from my first visit to your lovely home. Yes, I know that, as a lawyer, I should not jump to such conclusions. It's unprofessional, especially for a lawyer. However, once I was aware of the idea of a cult, the correlations were far too similar. I don't know how aware you are of the history of the Women's Health Corps, but for the past few decades, they have been less a matter of pro-choice and largely anti-Life. Even if there wasn't actual Moloch worship involved, I would conclude that they were akin to a cult without the formality. A spree of incidents across the country tells me that people like Kermit Gosnell are less an aberration and more of a trend. Forced abortions? Underage abortions? Unsanitary working conditions. It tells me that they are less interested in a right to choose and more interested in an obligation to die." He looked to Father Freeman. "I presume that you have heard of such things?"

Freeman smiled. "I have given the odd lecture about it."

"To us, most recently," Alex said as he came in the door. "So, how bad is everything?"

"We just started," I told him.

Carlton nodded. "You see, the entire problem of the WHC is that they don't have anything to do with health. While not officially— read, 'publicly'—affiliated with them, the WHC is supported by many academics who back certain movements frowned upon by civilized human beings. They support child murder and putting down the elderly before they take 'too many resources' from everyone else. To say that they are monstrous does a grave injustice to actual monsters. Doctor Victor Frankenstein did not create his monster and then demand he be subsidized by the villagers. Jack the Ripper did not go to the local 'good government' groups and insist that he be reimbursed for his efforts in cleaning up the hookers of the West End. The WHC had created a culture where more black children are aborted in New York than are born alive, and then boast about their *service* to the black community, and to tamper with said service is tantamount to racism—then they demand city, state, and federal funding. Somehow, they have murdered more 'lesser breeds' than the Nazis or the Klan, and yet they call their opposition are Nazis and Klansmen. I have seen more compassion, sense, and remorse from men whom I have recommended sentences of twenty-five to life.

"And now, your task becomes even more difficult. You have already run into the various and sundry levels of political protection that they have. The Mayor will fight to the death to keep them intact. They are the lifeblood of the party, if you will pardon the expression.

Merely having the truck go into LaObliger's neighborhood will not be enough for a warrant. No one will grant it at my office. If I apply for it, you can be certain that I will be either fired, suspended, or pilloried in the press until I can be forced into a public apology for even considering it. We are at the point where the only method of political discourse is via whatever works on the lesser parts of the Internet. To say it is disappointing would be underestimating it to such an extent, it would be insulting.

"To even canvas the neighborhood of King's Point would probably be enough to alert LaObliger, and thus the mayor, to your activities, and have you branded as misusing the force of the police department to harass...health professionals," he growled in disdain. "So you can see that you have a slight problem to deal with. You know that LaObliger is actually behind what is after you and your family. Given the powers involved, do you truly wish to sit back, relax, and wait for them to come to you? How would you catch them? How would I prosecute them—assuming that I would even be allowed? How could you possibly hope to touch them? Some sort of undercover sting would require paperwork. Which would go through the chain of command, and it would reach Mayor Hoynes, who would once again run interference for the Women's Health Corps."

I shrugged. "Do you have another option?"

Alex gave a harsh laugh. "We could go all *Lethal Weapon* on them. Kill all of them. Let's face it, we could probably talk to D. I don't think he'd like these people, either."

Mariel, Freeman and I looked at him like he had lost his mind.

"Really?" I asked. "Are you kidding me, Alex?"

Alex shrugged. "You have a better idea?"

"We have to be patient," I told him. "Do the work. Stake out some of these abortion mills. Wait for a fake truck to come along. We tail it to LaObliger's house, then ask her what she's doing with all of those body parts. Heck, we can stake out her house and see when one shows up. Who's to say they're not getting a truckload delivered to her house once a week, or once a day? We only know about one abortion mill they've taken from. Perhaps there were others. We could have her arrested within the month. Perhaps within the week."

Freeman nodded. "I hate to interject but going on a mission to assassinate LaObliger would be especially problematic for the state of Tom's soul. Right now, one of the few advantages that you have lies in his abilities. The moment you resolve to slaughter is the moment where those abilities would likely go away."

"Exactly. We need to be patient. We need to do the work, put in the time, and *then* get them."

Carlton's great head nodded, almost as though he approved of the attitude. "That is an admirable mindset. And I would applaud it if not for one thing—how many times have you been under direct attack in the last forty-eight hours alone?"

My old house. Bellevue. The morgue. The abortion mill in South Jamaica. Poisoning in Nassau. Attack on my new house. "Six."

Carlton's eyebrows rose. "So not only does this plan assume that you can operate for as long as a month without someone catching you and setting up political roadblocks, but it must also assume that you can survive attacks that come at you at least once every eight hours. Have you considered increasing your life insurance?"

"I have," Alex answered. "Ever since a demon threw chairs at me with his mind."

I rolled my eyes. "Father Freeman said it—my abilities have given me enough of an edge to keep me alive thus far. I just need to stay alive long enough to make a case." I looked back and forth between the ADA and my partner. "Come on, people. Alex and I managed to arrest a serial killer possessed by a *demon* back in September. What part of 'with God, all things are possible' escapes you two? HE's had our backs so far against a supernatural scourge. And you think that casual slaughter is going to fix it? No. We have to Do the Job."

I threw my hands into the air, exasperated. The tie felt like it was choking me, and it was a clip-on. I pulled it out and undid the top button. "Gah! All right, I need to get out of these clothes. At least the shirt. You folks ... just talk among yourselves."

I went for the stairs ... and stopped. The scent of evil that lingered in the air had gotten stronger. Even though the Bokor and his zombies hadn't come near the stairs. I took a few steps up, and the smell increased.

Jeremy.

I bounded up the stairs two at a time, and I heard Alex come up behind me. I charged straight for my son's room and shouldered the door open with a crash.

The bed was empty. The sheets had been thrown to one side of the room. There was a knife driven to the hilt in the pillows, pinning them to the bed. It anchored a wide sheet of paper to the pillows.

It read, "If you want your son, you know where to go."

Chapter 19

TAKEN

They had my son.

Outside of being shot at, I rarely had that sensation where my focus telescoped to one narrow corridor of panic. In that instant, there was nothing in the world that mattered more than getting my son back. To kill in defense of one's loved ones was possibly the oldest law of acceptable violent behavior. Call it natural law. Call it the law of the jungle. Either way, it didn't require an in-depth knowledge of the catechism to conclude that anyone who tried to harm Jeremy was going to either surrender quietly or die screaming.

Granted, there was a large angry part of me that hoped that the kidnappers didn't want, or try to, surrender, but that part had to be pushed aside and pressed down. Alex, and even Carlton's, solution of "kill them all" wouldn't help. Even if that turned out to be the end result, Jeremy had to be secured first, above all else. The logical side of my mind realized that, yes, the day may end with no arrests. But Jeremy came first.

Then we could see if anyone wanted to surrender before the shootout started.

Alex barged in behind me, gun drawn and expecting another creature to shoot. He saw the note. "You know where to go?"

I nodded calmly. "Of course. They know we have Borgia. They know we can trace the truck. They may even know that we have already. It's LaObliger."

"But we have no way of knowing that."

I nodded slowly, strangely calm and detached. "Because that would mean we can't go without a tactical team. We know but can't prove. That means we have no grounds. We have to do this ourselves. They know that. It's what they want. No SWAT, ESU, and if we play this even a little out of line, they'll kill Jeremy."

Alex sighed and put his gun away. "*Now* can we kill them all?"

"After a fashion," I hedged. "Let's tell Mariel."

Alex scoffed. "Better you than me, buddy."

We went downstairs. Mariel waited at the bottom landing, shotgun at the ready. "Well?"

I explained, calmly, gently, softly, the note and the condition of the bedroom. Freeman and Carlton listened in the living room. The ADA wisely said nothing. Freeman blessed himself.

Mariel's eyes narrowed. "How and when are we getting him back?"

I checked my watch. "Give me a few minutes. Then we'll head right out and get him."

Mariel blinked, surprised. "That fast?"

I shrugged. "No time like the present."

She looked at me strangely. "Don't the people at the station need more time to mobilize?"

"I'm not going to the station." I looked to ADA Carlton. "Could you explain while I open the gun safe?"

"Gladly." Carlton sighed. He leaned forward with his great lumbering mass and began to pontificate. "Right now, the message as described, gives us no probable cause to go for anyone in particular. No one has claimed responsibility, and thus we have no door to knock down. We cannot prove anything. We may be close to a warrant or a SWAT team in a dire emergency, but we have nothing that can stand up to the political pressure and cover being given by the mayor. We cannot preclude an informant for City Hall within the station. If we attempt to attain anyone's assistance within the department, not only will we most likely inform the mayor about the raid, but also his good friend, President LaObliger would hear soon after. We would gain nothing and—pardon my bluntness—but most likely lose everything, namely Jeremy. The political protection LaObliger has is a nightmare.

"If you wish me to be honest, the only way that we can get a *legal* method for Detective Nolan to enter LaObliger's abode would be for him to be invited into her residence, see illegal activity, call in backup, and hopefully await the reinforcements and survive long enough for them to arrive. May I respectfully suggest that if the kidnappers let him anywhere near Jeremy, they will undoubtedly search him for any and all listening communication devices.

"Normally, the best way to do that would be via a laser microphone from a van across the street. But, again, it is unlikely. The FBI has such a device, but good luck contacting the federal authorities, coordinating with them, and stirring them to action before it makes it back to the mayor. Or, worse, have the FBI act fast enough to be of any assistance at all.

"In short, you will not get anyone with law enforcement to help you. Not in the time frame you have to work with."

"And we won't," I told them. "Come on. Let's go."

Mariel blinked, confused. "Where?"

"We're going to get our son back."

To say that King's Point is the nice part of Long Island doesn't quite capture it. To start with, you have to find it first. There's a little white-letters-on-green-background sign that meekly says "King's Point," as a way of guiding people who know what they're looking for. But if you don't know they exist, they do not want you in the neighborhood. If you're driving by King's Point, along Community Drive, which starts just off of the Long Island Expressway, you'll see trees. There will be plenty of tall, lush trees, covering the very existence of the area. It could be mistaken for all of the flora that covered the sides of the highways. There is only the barest occasional hint that there is something behind the trees. At the right angle during the winter, when the trees are bare, you can catch glimpses of fine six-bedroom homes and wide arcing driveways, the occasional brownstone or bay window.

To turn into King's Point is to enter the land of *The Great Gatsby*, Great Neck (instead of "Big Egg"). The homes were closer to old-fashioned mansions than the McMansions that arose in the late nineties. The homes were varied, but many had optional extras of varying sorts. Some had extra pieces of land that made for one heck of a front yard. Some had tennis courts and swimming pools that were jealously guarded by a chain link fence (No barbed wire, it isn't *that* sort of neighborhood). At a wrong turn, one could unknowingly drive up someone's driveway, mistaking it for a street. Some homes were cut off from the others by an additional bodyguard of trees, isolating themselves from their neighbors. If one stuck to the outer perimeter of King's Point, one would find that every cul-de-sac oversaw the water. Many of the homes at the end of the cul-de-sac had docks and boats in their backyards.

The only people who made less than six figures a year in that neighborhood were the gardeners ...and to be honest, I wasn't even going to consider the size of their tips or the rates they charged. For all I knew, they were in the upper-middle-class neighborhood down the street.

King's Point at night remained idyllic. In areas where the street lamps might be insufficient, the external lights of all the homes lit the streets and the walkways, welcoming any and all in the streets to the town.

It short, it looked nice. Some homes were more obviously wealthy than others, but most were subdued and remained low key, unpretentious and not flashy. For the most part, it was what small business owners aspired to—nice home, nice neighborhood, a place to raise the kids without a problem.

It was here that the dragon's den was parked. I could almost see the truck of baby parts pull up to the house, and LaObliger passing it off as the weekly BBQ party with friends from work.

Sort of true.

President LaObliger's house was in one cul-de-sac that backed into the water. It was a two-story home, and the backyard leading to the water was cut off by trees and a high fence. The home was brown slate. There were two balconies in the front, and at least one more looking over the backyard. All three had two men on it, casually chatting away, as though they were there for a dinner party. Perhaps they were. It was obvious that I was going to be outgunned unless I carried a rocket-propelled grenade. Those things were heavy, so that was out of the question.

I was dropped off at the opening of the cul-de-sac. I walked on the opposite side of the street from her house. I wanted to look at the layout as I approached. The men on the balcony were probably armed. I half expected AKs, to be honest. Though that was a little too obvious. There were other people on the street, including some kids playing. A sight I'm sure Alex would have snarked about.

Shooting me would be difficult to explain to the neighbors.

Though, given the nature of LaObliger's people, I suspect there was a sacrificial knife with my name on it.

Chapter 20

LION'S DEN

As discussed, there was no way for me to get a warrant for LaObliger's home. Legally, I couldn't even so much as consider kicking the door in. There was only one way for me to enter her home.

I knocked.

I waited for a long moment. The front lawn was cut off from the sidewalk by tall bushes. Maybe someone directly across the street could see me, but aside from that, I could have been killed at that exact moment, and no one would have noticed.

As Alex told me before I left for this appointment in Samarra, "Dude, you are just *so* screwed."

Probably.

The door opened smoothly and soundlessly. Standing in the doorway was the tall black fellow from the morgue and the last attack on my house. He still wore the full suit and tie from earlier.

He grinned with the unnaturally bright white teeth that almost seemed to split his head open. He gave an elegant bow that gave me the impression that he was some sort of dancer. "Good evening, Detective. Welcome. I see you got our message."

"It was hard to miss." My eyes narrowed and I slowly, calmly asked, "Where is my son?"

He did nothing but step out of the doorway and wave me through. Given that he seemed to be the heavy in the voodoo department, it seemed strange that he was acting the part of the butler.

I walked through the hall, which led into the living room. It was wide and spacious, an open-floor plan that barely had any separation between rooms. Some of the makes and models of furniture were so high-end, I couldn't even identify them. The Swarovski chandelier and the Waterford glasses were the low end of the spectrum, from what I could tell.

And the room was full. Armed gunmen lined the walls. One wall of French doors faced the water, but I could barely see the water for the gunmen. I don't mean "they had a gun in a holster"; they were armed to the teeth. Each of them had ten handguns in holsters, and each of them had at least one long gun that I could see. If they were going to go that far into overkill, I was certain that there had to be at least two extra handguns kicking around as well. I couldn't imagine why they needed shotguns, especially considering how short most of the sightlines were. Unless they thought someone was coming in from the water, but that's what the Coast Guard is for.

There were two love seats, a full couch that reclined, and an armchair. The armchair was left unoccupied.

Right across from it was WHC President LaObliger.

I casually strolled towards the armchair. One of the armed guards stepped forward and patted me down.

"If you get any more thorough, you can buy me flowers. But my wife would object."

The gunman stopped, stared at me, and blinked, as though not understanding what I had said.

I shrugged. He finished and backed off. I strode down two steps to the main floor of the living room. I threw myself into the chair and leaned back.

"So, LaBitch, where is my son?"

"Call me that one more time, I'll have your son filleted."

I raised my eyebrow. "How about you tell me what you want so we can just get this over with?"

She shook her head. "Do you think that we're stupid? Or are you even dumber than we thought?"

I merely shrugged. "Where's Jeremy?"

LaObliger smiled, smug. "He's close."

"What's the game plan here? Kill me, then let him go? Or kill both of us and move on?"

LaObliger cocked her head, confused, like it was an odd question. "Kill you, yes. Move on, no."

I looked around at the circle of armed men. "What was all of this about? Are you really that pissed about me driving off your demon?"

LaObliger smiled evilly. "We don't believe in justice, Detective Nolan. We don't even believe in simple payback. We believe in *revenge*. We will kill you, and then we'll kill your son. Eventually, we'll kill your wife. And yes, you did get in our way with the demon. Do you know how hard it is to control one of those things without it turning around and biting you on the ass?"

I folded my hands in front of me, trying to be casual. "Very, I imagine. Especially since the last time I checked, there was only one rule book that could put a demon away once you summon it and that happens to belong to the Catholic church. If you slipped up once, you'd be the one on the menu."

She nodded. "Exactly."

I arched a brow and looked over to the side, where the Bokor glided behind LaObliger. "You mean he didn't do it for you?"

LaObliger blinked and looked over her shoulder at him. "Oh, Mr. Baracus, you mean? Oh no, only his master did that."

I blinked, only a little surprised. I thought back to the padded cell with Rene Ormeno. "You mean the warlock?"

For the first time, the Bokor stopped smiling, and LaObliger looked at me like she was going to have me skinned immediately.

"Who told you about him?" she snapped.

I casually shrugged. "I heard it through the grapevine." I shook my head. "So, what made you people decide to voluntarily join the forces of evil?"

LaObliger froze for a moment then burst out into a bout of intense laughter, doubling over in her chair. When she came up, gasping for air, she had tears in her eyes. "Evil? Oh, please, Detective. Moloch isn't *evil*. There is no such *thing* as good and evil, didn't you *know* that?" She sighed. "Oh, you Catholics and your simplistic good/evil dichotomy."

Not bad. I wouldn't have guessed she'd know what dichotomy meant.

"We merely dispose of the unwanted and unloved," LaObliger continued. "We cremate their remains, and we profit. *Everyone* in the cult has seen their profits rise beyond *all* imagining, as long as the sacrifices keep coming."

Except the sacrifices are baby body parts? Do you people even listen to yourselves? I said, "You realize he's a demon? Right?"

She waved it away. "Feh. You Catholics and your labels. He is the god of money! He will support us forever! As long as we support him. We will keep him fed, you know. Forever and ever. And he will give us everything that we require. Money will come to us and, with the money, power. The power to control politicians. Power to control laws. Power to legislate what's right and wrong."

"Uh huh. I should listen to the demonologist about morality?"

LaObliger scoffed. "Please. Your old-fashioned system is anti-quated. We're talking about *true* morality. Like outlawing cigarettes or allowing little people like you to have guns. We've outlawed transfats, so the next step is real fat. Even fat people. We've...*allowed you people*," she said with disdain, "a few more years to worship as you see fit. But soon, we'll have the power to rule that Churches like yours are child abuse."

I arched my brows at that. It didn't occur to me that they would be quite that..."moral," I guess. For lack of a better term.

"There's a reason that CS Lewis stated that of all tyrannies, a tyranny sincerely exercised for the good of its victims may be the most oppressive. Those who torment us for our own good will torment us without end for they do so with the approval of their own conscience."

LaObliger laughed in my face. "But we are doing it for everyone's own good. Don't you understand?"

I didn't even want to try getting into that ball pit of crazy with her. "Seriously, though? Why summon the demon with Curran?"

LaObliger rolled her eyes. "We're not going to waste *all* of our time explaining things to you. Mister Baracus, if you please?"

I flinched. "Baracus?"

He smiled. In his lyrical accent, he introduced himself. "Bokor Baracus. At your service, Detective. For now."

I rolled my eyes. "Of course." I looked back to LaObliger. "Was that *it*? All this was about a revenge scheme for foiling your demon?" I waved around the room. "Of all these people, do you think that you could have used your resources for more...I don't know...profitable ventures?"

LaObliger shook her head. "Oh please. There's nothing we hate more than some prick who thinks he's a do-gooder. You think you're so pure and so virtuous when there isn't even any such thing as good or evil. You need to be destroyed because you're a symbol. You're the myth of something good. And good isn't real. But power is. And what good is power if you can't use it every once in a while?"

I stared at her for a long moment, blankly. I had trouble wrapping my brain around this insanity. "So you did all of this just because you could?"

"Exactly," LaObliger growled. "I've had enough. Get up, Nolan. You're taking a walk."

The guns came up, and the Bokor smiled again. I shrugged and rose to my feet.

Now, you're probably wondering, *Why is Nolan so calm*? I was doing the rosary in my head the entire time. From the moment I headed for King's Point to the moment they told me to get up. I could be nervous, or I could be focused. I preferred focused. I knew God was on my side this time, and I was leaning heavily on Him to pick up the slack. If He wasn't, I would have been in *real* trouble...

Not that I wasn't. But I was almost certain that I was going to die tonight. Given how their demon had cut up his victims in the manner similar to a partial-birth abortion, if my body was found in fewer than a dozen parts, I would have gotten off easy.

But it didn't matter what happened to me. Jeremy was the only thing that mattered. He would be coming out the other end of this. In fact, the best outcome for the evening that I could guess what would involve my bullet-ridden corpse. Yes, my best plan involved my death. Saving Jeremy wasn't the most important thing. It was the *only* thing.

The backyard was quite nice. The French doors opened out into a concrete patio with a layout for a dinner party. I didn't want to ask what was usually on the menu.

The rest of the backyard was an extensive, perfect grassy lawn that sloped down to the sound. It terminated at the water's edge, with full, tall, lush topiary bushes that cut off some of the view.

The bushes were most likely designed to hide the twelve-foot statue of the demon Moloch from the outside world, like passing boats and neighbors. The great hulking, flat-black basalt statue looked like an angry bipedal bull.

A few feet away, in front of the statue was a large, deep fire pit, with the flame raging out of control, occupying most of the inside surface. The angry red light from the flickering flame bounced off the glinting surface of the swimming pool not far away.

The light from the flames below gave the black statue the aspect of rising directly from Hell.

In between the fire pit and the statue, hogtied and sprawled out on the ground, was my son Jeremy. He saw me and thrashed against his restraints.

That was more than enough.

I stopped walking about halfway on the grass. I turned to face ... all of them. There had to be at least thirty gunmen I could see. There were probably at least fifty total throughout the grounds. All of their guns were at the ready, in case I bolted for it.

I kept my breathing calm and even, still going through the rosary in my head.

I looked at all of them, meeting their eyes—as many as I could. Empty were the eyes of everyone. They were all dead inside. There was no repentance. There was no hesitation. They had gone from baby parts of the aborted to a fully-grown child, and they were no longer phased by cold-blooded murder, assuming they ever were.

Funny enough, just like Curran.

I squared my feet, clasped my hands behind my back in parade ground rest, and said, in a voice as clear and as strong as I could broadcast, "You are all under arrest. Would any of you like to surrender, or are you all going to resist?"

Chapter 21

SLAYING THE DRAGON

After a moment of stunned silence, LaObliger started laughing. So did the gunmen near her. So did everyone around her.

Bokor Baracus was the only one not laughing. His smile had dropped. He looked at me like I was up to something. That just proved that he was the smartest one then.

LaObliger pointed at me and barked, "Burn him! Burn his son and make him watch!"

Five men started forward.

I raised my hand in a bit of theatricality. "Stay right there, or I will kill you with a snap of my fingers."

The gunmen stopped, confused. LaObliger sneered. "You don't have that power."

"Are you sure?" I smiled. "After all, if you could summon a demon, why can't I be able to do supernatural hoodoo?"

The Bokor, Baracus, put his hand on her shoulder, his long fingers encompassing much of her arm. "Be care-ful," he sang.

LaObliger jerked her arm away from the Bokor, eyes narrowed and angry. "Shut up, you stupid nigger. You're to do everything I tell you to. That was the deal."

The Bokor raised his hands and stepped back. "As you wish."

LaObliger growled and reached under the patio table. She yanked out a large knife, perhaps even a machete. It was ornate and almost ceremonial. "I'll do it myself. Men, with me."

The five men who had been hesitant marched alongside her.

It was obvious that I couldn't delay any longer. I raised my hand and snapped my fingers.

All five gunmen died in the first volley of gunfire. At the same time, gunfire burst out at the front of the house. LaObliger hit the deck, and the other gunmen jerked up and around, startled by the sudden attack. The sound of a speedboat cut through the air as automatic fire opened up, spraying the tightly-packed gunmen who had been there just to handle me. Bullets from half a dozen guns riddled them.

D and his crew had arrived.

I did two things at once.

In LaObliger's backyard, I dashed for Jeremy the moment the gunmen were occupied with the gunfire.

Outside, in the car I arrived in, I was also there. I had bilocated before the car stopped and exited onto the street while also driving away. The other me had been what I had used to call out. Since I'm the same person, no matter where I was, or how many places I was, I knew everything that I knew. The moment I saw Jeremy in the backyard, I called out from the car, calling everyone to move in. And I did want to offer them at least the opportunity to give up. But everything I said from then on was merely a distraction.

However, the moment I made the call for backup, the duplicate me ceased to be. My vision had collapsed into one. My backup had arrived. God apparently didn't think I needed more than that. I'd trust to his tactical judgment.

As I ran for Jeremy, I didn't hesitate, even as the bullets zipped past my ears and ate up the ground around my feet. I wasn't ungrateful, but I was surprised. I was at relatively short range, especially for that amount of hardware. Were they blind or just really bad shots, or

...

Were they hired because they were cult members, not because they're actual gunslingers by profession?

I ran around the fire pit and made it to Jeremy He was restrained with zip ties. I didn't have a knife on me. I didn't even have a weapon. This was the part of the plan that was all on God. Because my plan was simple—until reinforcements could get to me, shield Jeremy with my body and hope the bullets didn't go through me. My coat was a dark gray, and the smoke from the fire pit covered us. If we were lucky, they'd keep me covered.

So, of course, the wind changed and blew the smoke away, revealing both of us clearly.

Oh my God, I am heartily sorry that I have offended thee—

Machinegun fire went off near me, and I started. Since I didn't feel anything, I looked up.

D's men were right next to me and charging forward. Alex and Mariel stopped next to me. Alex had Jeremy's AR-15. I knew it was his because it was wrapped in a pattern of the stars and stripes. Mariel had hers out, wrapped in pink, and handed me mine. I took it with a nod then whirled on the gunmen, who were scattered and leaderless, and uncoordinated.

D's men moved forward, blasting away in short bursts of automatic fire. Unlike us, they weren't using semi-automatic rifles but weapons that were probably illegal in New York State... I wasn't a lawyer, nor was I proficient in the myriad rules and regulations that made up the gun laws of my state, so I'd say it was wise to just err on the side of caution. Give them the benefit of the doubt...at least, that's what I would say if I lived to file a report on this.

"Where'd you come from?" I asked between gunfire.

"There's a dock down by the water," Alex answered. He fired three more rounds in three different directions. "We just came up in the speedboat."

I frowned, spotted someone else, and fired twice. "How'd you know there would be a dock?"

"The tie on the black guy," Alex called back. *Bang bang.* "The crosshairs on his tie? Not crosshairs. It's a nautical symbol."

I frowned, puzzled, as I clocked another one and shot him. "What do you know of boats?"

Bang bang bang. "I hope to live long enough to retire on one. Assuming you don't get me killed first."

"Really? I always thought you were joking."

"About buying a boat?"

"About retiring."

I glanced down to check Mariel's progress. As I expected, she had a knife out and ready, cutting Jeremy loose from his bonds.

When I had developed the plan, it didn't take me long. Perhaps it was logic. Perhaps God just gave me the plan whole and entire. As ADA Carlton said, we couldn't get a warrant or a SWAT team to break down LaObliger's door, especially not with the evidence we had balanced against the political cover she had. We needed exigent circumstances, evidence of an immediate risk to someone's life. I could get that once I was inside and found Jeremy. But we all knew that I would be searched for listening devices. That was solved by bilocation.

Unfortunately, that also meant that both Jeremy and I would be minutes from death, and the SWAT team would take a few minutes longer than we would have.

So D and his gang would have to operate as our backup. Mariel would join in to get Jeremy away. It would be her only job.

Meanwhile, as soon as I called in the danger signal, ADA Carlton would call in the Nassau County Police and their SWAT team—they were outside of Mayor Hoynes's influence.

The gunfight moved closer to the house as the resistance waned. LaObliger's gunmen had retreated back into the building and were going to make it a matter of room-to-room fighting. They didn't know that we didn't care about what they wanted to do. D's people were merely going to hold them inside the building and wait for the SWAT team. That way, D's gunmen on both ends would disappear into the background of King's Point, and SWAT would provide the cleanup.

D wandered by, shotgun in hand. He looked over the backyard battleground and shook his head. "Pity. Nice looking place for—" He stopped and looked above us at the statue of Moloch. "Okay, that's butt ugly. But otherwise, not bad. It even has a BBQ pit."

D blinked, frowned, and looked from Moloch to the pit and back. He looked over at me and said, "I don't want to know what's been in there, do I?"

I shook my head. "No. No, you don't."

He frowned. "I figured."

"There you go!" Mariel cried as the last of Jeremy's bonds fell away. She hugged him close.

Without warning, a fresh burst of gunfire opened up on us from the house. The French windows burst open on the lower floor, and the balcony above also. It was strange and coordinated and sudden.

We took cover as best we could, some behind the Moloch statue...until we realized that the rest of D's forces were being shot at.

They don't want to hit the statue.

I returned fire, as did D and Alex. It was strange, I had a feeling of deja vu.

Then I realized what the problem really was. Many of the positions that had opened up with new gunfire were from people I had already shot and killed. It was as though they had a second wind.

Or, more accurately, they had come back from the dead.

"Zombie gunman!" I barked at them.

D looked at me like I had lost my mind. "You gotta be kidding me."

"It's Voodoo. They have a Bokor."

D narrowed his eyes at me. "Mister Tall, Dark, and Overdressed? I clocked him earlier. He seemed like a minion."

"After a fashion. You're going to have to do more than blow their heads off. You're going to have to dismember them as long as the Bokor is on site."

D frowned then pulled out his cell phone. It chirped. "Okay, boys. We've got the zombie apocalypse, and they have guns. It's less *Resident Evil* and more *Dead Space*. Ben, I know you have your Bowie knife, so go play. Let's go to work, people." He lowered the radio and spared Alex a glance. "I thought it was odd when his wife told me to bring rock-salt shells. Now I guess I know why, huh?"

Alex scoffed. "Welcome to my world, dude."

Then Women's Health Corps President LaObliger jumped out of the bushes with her insanely large knife and came at my wife and son.

Chapter 22

REVENGE OF THE DEAD

LaObliger was too close for Mariel to shoot her with the AR-15. Instead, Mariel swung the rifle around to intercept the blade. Mariel could have deflected the blade as it came down and shot LaObliger in the torso. But the knife came up, under the barrel, and slashed at Mariel's stomach. She hollowed out, sucking her gut in and away from the knife. That left the rifle up over her head. LaObliger stabbed straight for Mariel's stomach. She pivoted out of the way, letting the knife pass her.

Mariel brought the butt of her AR down onto LaObliger's wrist. It shattered with a crunch. Mariel smacked her in the mouth with the side of the rifle and shoved her away with the gun stock. Mariel brought her knee up and kicked LaObliger away.

She pointed her rifle at LaObliger. The President of the WHC raised her hands, and said, "I surrender."

"My husband is the cop," Mariel said.

Then she fired two rounds into LaObliger's stomach. Before she could crumple, Mariel took two steps forward and grabbed LaObliger by the shirt. "You kidnapped my son. You tried to murder my husband. Guess what, bitch? My husband may be a saint. I'm not."

Mariel let go of the shirt and gave LaObliger a hard shove.

LaObliger fell backwards into the fire pit. Even over the hail of gunfire, I could hear LaObliger scream all the way down.

It sounded like she fell for a very long time.

The flames turned a pale, sickly green, as though LaObliger were covered in flaming copper. And it didn't stop burning green until the screaming stopped.

Mariel spat into the fire pit. "Burn in hell, bitch."

Normally, at this point in an action film, the hero would at least be able to express some satisfaction in the death of someone who was, let's face it, straightforward evil. As a Catholic, I was disappointed that she wasn't redeemable. As a cop, I was worried I'd have even more paperwork to fill out. As a father, I was happy she was one less problem to cope with as the bullets kept coming for me. But I can definitely tell you that the air smelled a heck of a lot sweeter the moment she fell in. And just maybe her death would lead to fewer murdered children.

Okay, I was at least relieved that she was dead.

Alex cackled as LaObliger fell in. "She was never the same since the house fell on her sister."

As the green glow from the fire died off, several of D's men pulled back, wounded. The zombie gunmen were starting to recover ground.

"Mariel, run!" I barked. "We may have to settle for getting out of here."

While she and Jeremy made a break for it, D, Alex and I pushed forward, firing left, right, and center. Bullets wouldn't kill the zombies, but they would slow them down a second, which was enough time for one of us to put two more bullets in their heads— which slowed them down even further.

One thing I didn't tell Mariel is that SWAT wouldn't be able to handle the zombies. They wouldn't know what to do with them, especially not fast enough to survive. We did.

And we plowed into them. It was a simple pattern. I shot a zombie in the head, rending some of the senses useless. Alex kneecapped it so it couldn't walk. D jammed the shotgun into the zombie's armpit to disarm him, so to speak. D kicked the arm and the weapon away, I kicked the zombie out of the way, and we were off.

Only once we got a certain measure away from the Moloch statue, the heavy fire drove us back to within its protective shadow. D's wounded were also gathering there. It looked like the wounded were starting to outnumber the healthy ones.

"We can't get to the zombies," I said. "And they and the rest of the WHC gunmen only need to hold the house. A SWAT team would be taken out if it's just them versus zombies."

D looked at me cynically. "Do you have any ideas, Detective? Because I don't see how we can taunt zombies to come and get us."

I shook my head. "We don't need to piss off the zombies. We need to piss off the Bokor controlling them. We need something he might care about or want ..."

I drifted off. We had something he wanted—me. And we had something he might even care about. We were using it for cover.

"Hey, D, shoot the statue. In the face, if you can."

D looked at me like I was nuts. "Why?"

"They don't want it damaged. So maybe damaging it will make them come to us." I looked at the others. "Everyone who's wounded, fall back. This is going to get worse before it gets better."

They didn't argue with me.

As soon as the first man started to run, Alex and I laid down cover fire for their retreat. Once the final one got away, we kept firing, letting D shoot the statue.

The night was suddenly filled with loud, angry growls. It was almost like we had been surrounded by the world's worst junkyard dogs.

Alex gave me a look and shrugged. "I think we got their attention."

I furrowed my brows in thought. "Hey, D, back here. Shoot it in the back, so they can't see it."

D looked at me funny. "What will that do?"

"I want to see if they watched you do it, or if they felt it."

He shrugged, and fired.

The growling intensified.

I exchanged a look with Alex and D. "They felt that."

D grinned. "This is one of the places of power for the Voodoo man. I don't know if we can cut his power source, but this will definitely cause a disturbance in the dark side."

Alex arched a brow and looked at D. "How do you know what?"

"Don't you read fantasy?"

I thought it over. This was where the trucks had come, week after week, with their "sacrifices." The statue was the focal point for the demon and the power it gained from worship. If they could have spread it around the city, they would have. It would have made more sense. It would have been easier to hide. They wouldn't have been caught so easily if they could have just placed it in a cave in the brambles of Central Park, or anywhere along the shore of Long Island. They kept coming back here, meaning that it was important to "feed" this particular demon at this particular statue.

"Everyone, fall back!" I ordered. "Get the heck out of here. If this doesn't work, we're in trouble."

D looked to his men and nodded. They took the hint and started backing up. D looked back to me. "Sorry, Detective, you're not the boss of me. I'm staying."

I shrugged. "Suit yourself."

Alex shrugged. "Great. Now what?"

"We tip the statue into the firepit."

D shrugged. "Sure, why not. Got an idea how?"

I winced. This was going to hurt. "Yeah. I do." I put my AR down and looked to D. "Cover me."

Alex wheeled right around the statue, and D wheeled left, pouring bullets into the new attackers. I didn't know if it was blind fire or if zombies were closing in, but I wasn't going to wait and ask.

Despite the height of the monstrosity, it wasn't broad everywhere. In fact, I was relatively certain that I could get both arms around its neck. Normally, that wouldn't help. I couldn't get leverage. I'd be stuck on the ground trying to push it over with D and Alex, and we'd be without cover.

Thankfully, I wasn't normal.

I started an Our Father and started to climb the statue. I didn't need the lift yet. I could climb it all right.

God answered my prayer quick enough. I levitated straight to the top of the statue in an eye blink. I grabbed the thing around its neck, like I was trying to strangle it.

Then I pushed…if you can call flying into the statue with constant force "pushing." I pushed with my body flat against it so I wouldn't exert pressure on only one part of my body. I didn't want to ram it with my shoulder and dislocate the shoulder.

Despite all of the thought I put into my positioning, it still felt more like I was being crushed against the statue rather than pushing it.

The gunfire came at my face fast and furious, and D and Alex returned fire.

I just needed to get this done, and then it would be fine. I wouldn't care if I was shot, or stabbed, or fell into the fire pit. I just needed this thing to *die*. It was going to go to Hell, even if I had to escort it there myself.

My ribs started to creak and give. My shoulder felt like it was going to pop out of its socket. Even my knees and ankles felt the pressure.

I knew at this moment that this was it. I was going to take this thing down, but I was going down with it. It was an exchange I would be happy to make.

A loud grinding noise filled the air. A loud sound of stone against stone. The statue shifted and moved towards the fire pit.

A bullet ripped through my arm. It was a graze, but one that tore through all of the flesh along the back of my left forearm.

I ground my teeth and kept shoving. The bullets zinged by my head, singed hairs on my head, and clipped my shoulder, but I kept at it.

And then it tilted on its own.

A bullet clipped my head, knocking me senseless. I couldn't focus on anything. All I could feel was the sense that I was falling.

Chapter 23

BURNING THE DRAGON

I came to with Alex smacking me lightly on the cheek.

I opened my eyes with a start. The sound of gunfight sounded like it was coming through a tin drum. The sound was muffled and distant. My ears rang. I tried to push myself up, but Alex held me down. He didn't say anything, but pointed.

The statue had fallen...and hung over the fire pit, held up by the horns on top. The horns kept him in place by inches, but it was enough.

We were now exposed, without the statue's cover. Alex had dragged me over to the base of the statue, which meant there was about three feet of cover for all of us, and shrinking.

I grabbed my rifle, and rolled over, flat on my belly, and fired for the horns atop Moloch's head.

Every gunman standing (and most obviously dead) ran, crawled, and aimed at me. Thankfully, zombies were apparently piss poor shots, since the dirt around me exploded, but I wasn't hit.

"—hell with this," I heard D scream. He threw something over his head, and it struck the back of the statue's head.

Then the grenade exploded, blasting the head right off the Moloch statue. Without the head, the base was still at the edge of the fire pit, sending the object of LaObliger's worship straight into the flames, swinging down like a pendulum. It went down with a screaming, screeching crash, right into the fire.

The zombies stopped and stutter-stepped, as though their strings had been jerked, hard.

Then the zombies started to scream. They thrashed and jerked as though they were having seizures. Then, without warning, they all burst into flame... Just like the statue. Chunks of flaming stone sizzled as if it were a living thing, and the sound of keening was like the worst tinnitus broadcast on loudspeaker. I couldn't tell if it was the zombies, the sound of the stone itself breaking down in the heat, or the demon shrieking in defeat.

I groaned and tried to push myself to my feet. I fell back into the dirt. Alex grabbed my healthy arm and yanked me to my feet. "Come on, let's go."

I hobbled to my feet. I barely knew where I was at the moment, only that it was time to go. I barely felt the blood running down my face like a half-mask. I tried to run my fingers through my hair, and they came back with blood. For a moment, I couldn't even remember how I started bleeding.

D swept the area over the sights of his shotgun, and nodded, satisfied that the zombies were gone.

Unfortunately, that's when Bokor Baracus jumped out of thin air (possibly the bushes, and I didn't see him) and clubbed D over the head with the pommel of a huge Bowie knife.

Alex tried to balance me and aim with the rifle at the same time. The Bokor darted in, low and quick. Alex only got off a single round before Baracus closed. Baracus slap-kicked the rifle to one side, then kicked Alex away. Since Alex supported me, I came tumbling after. I tried to move my rifle into position, but it was pinned under Alex. I rolled away from Alex, hoping that the movement would distract from my partner.

I rolled into the bushes.

I scrambled to my feet as the blade came in. I jerked back at the glint of the knife, and it slashed open my chin. I was up against a solid wall of bush. Baracus grabbed me by the shirt and jammed his knife against my throat. His bright white teeth shone clearly in the dark. "While I do not mind your meddling, Detective, I *do* mind destroying the power I accumulated here."

Normally, I would have shrugged. I might have even apologized for the inconvenience. But my head was so scrambled, I could only chuckle. I wasn't sure if I found him funny or just laughed at all of the witty comebacks I was too disoriented to say.

Baracus tilted his head, like a dog hearing a strange whistle. He shook me, one-handed, trying to get more of a reaction out of me.

"Bah!" He moved the knife away from my throat and smacked me across the face before he tossed me aside like a rag doll. "You're no *fun* in this condition."

He turned back to Alex, who was still sprawled out on the ground. He loomed over my partner, and laughed. "Maybe you will give me more sport."

Alex's eyes popped open, and his rifle came up, jamming into Baracus' stomach. "You want sport? How about target shooting."

He pulled the trigger.

The empty *click* never sounded so loud in my entire life.

Baracus grabbed the rifle and yanked it out of Alex's hands, hurling it aside as easily as he had mine. His foot came down on Alex's stomach, making him roll up into a ball. Baracus reached down and grabbed Alex by the collar of his coat, and dragged him towards the fire pit.

I pushed off of my feet, forcing myself to focus on Baracus. I needed to save Alex. Just as importantly, I needed to stop Baracus. I needed Baracus in jail. I needed him to talk. I needed him to get to LaObliger's benefactor, the warlock who raised the demon. Without Baracus, this nightmare could start all over again. He could move to a new city, a new organization, build a new cult. If he knew enough of the members of LaObliger's cult, he wouldn't even have to do much to start over.

I didn't have a gun.

But I had a backyard.

I grabbed a rock, reared back, and hurled it at Baracus. It bounced off of him like he was a wall. He gave me a passing glance, and smiled. "I will be with you in a minute, detective."

I growled in frustration and ran right for him. Baracus sighed, as though annoyed, and hurled Alex at me. We both went down in a tumble of arms and legs. I ended up on top and made it to my feet. The adrenaline had kicked in, and my vision tunneled in on Baracus. His knife came out, and he squared off with me.

Baracus beckoned me forward. "Come. Embrace your death, Detective."

I smiled at him as best as I could as I staggered towards him. "I'm only going to die tonight if God wants me to."

"Ah. But mine *does*."

I caught a glint of something on the ground. I gave him a genuinely amused scoff this time as I lurched forward. Blood ran down my face, tinting the vision in my left eye. I felt the blood run down my chin and stain my shirt. "You don't have a god. You have a demon. God created all. Sustains all. Allows everything to exist, even you."

I stopped within thirty feet of Baracus. He could probably close the distance in a second. I sagged and dropped to one knee, both of my hands on the ground. My hand landed on the object I spotted that glinted before. "And so, as the only person here who represents the good God Almighty, I will respectfully accept your surrender."

Baracus stepped forward calmly, casually. "I will respectfully decline."

I lifted my head to see him wind up with his knife, ready to kill me.

He swung.

I met his wrist with the edge of LaObliger's ceremonial blade, slashing his arm open, and knocking the blade away. I reversed my attack, slashing across his belly, but he leapt back before I could disembowel him.

He laughed like a maniac. "Oh! Ho ho ho ho! *That's* the spirit,

Detective. That's the fire I wanted to see before I extinguish you forever."

I pushed to my feet, knife in hand. My eyes narrowed. He'd had his chance. "Praise me to the Lord," I gasped. "My Rock," I lurched forward. "Who trains my hands for war and my fingers for battle."

Baracus closed. I swiped at him, and he batted the knife away easily. Before he could follow through, I burst forward, grabbed his perfectly immaculate suit by the labels, and rammed the crown of my forehead into his face. He wanted my blood? I'd happily bleed all over him.

My feet hit the ground, dragging him to my level. I drove my elbow in an uppercut to his chin, snapping his head back. My arm came down around his head, and I wrapped it around his neck in a headlock. "He is my loving God and my *fortress*," I intoned with a jerk to his head, trying to keep him in place. I positioned my legs so that I was closer to hurling him over my hip than pulling him in front of me —I didn't want to give him a clear shot between my legs. "My strong-hold and my deliverer! My shield, in whom I take refuge!"

I tried to throw him over, but he used his left arm to wrap around my leg from behind. He casually lifted me up and off the ground. He fell backwards, slamming the both of us into the ground. I held onto him during all of that. But now that we were on the ground, he'd have the advantage.

I broke the hold but grabbed his right ear so I could drive my left fist into his face. I rolled over on top of him. I mounted his chest and proceeded to pummel him with both hands.

"Who subdues peoples under me!" I bellowed, not getting the humor in the position I was in.

With inhuman strength, Baracus grabbed both of my wrists and pushed, throwing me off of him by several feet. I hit the ground in a roll and came to my feet next to Alex.

Lord, what are human beings that you care for them? Mere mortals that you think of them? They are like a breath; their days are like a fleeting shadow.

Baracus rose to his feet like he had been unaffected by everything

I had done to him. The only blood on him was mine. His nose wasn't even broken. He didn't have so much as a split lip. The fire from the still-burning pit illuminated him clearly. He had a twinkle in his eye, and a song in his heart—unfortunately, that song was from *Indiana Jones and the Temple of Doom.*

My breathing sped up. I was going to have to put him down soon. I looked down at my partner who was out cold. I needed to get between him and Baracus, lest he become a pawn in the fighting...

Then I spotted something on his belt. I dropped to a knee, grabbed it, and locked eyes with Baracus. The flames reflected in his eyes as though they were the source of the flames.

I charged. So did he. As we closed to a dozen paces, I leaped, fist cocked and ready, and wrapped around the tool from Alex's belt.

I punched Baracus right across the mouth, knuckles first, wrapped around the handle of Alex's collapsed tactical baton. Baracus flinched this time, his head snapping back, a tooth flying out of his mouth.

"*Part your heavens, Lord, and come down!*" I roared. I snapped open the baton and backhanded it across his head. "*Touch the mountains, so they smoke!*" I swept down with the baton, cracking it over his knees. "*Send forth lightning and scatter the enemy!*" The baton came up and down on the side of his skull. "*Shoot your arrows and rout them.*"

Baracus staggered forward several steps, shaken and unsteady. He straightened. His gaze was sharp, but I had split the skin of his scalp. His eyes were no longer amused but alight with rage. The flames roared behind me.

Baracus darted in, low and quick, like a Greco-Roman wrestler. His long left fingers wrapped around my wrist with the baton. His right hand came up and he punched me in the face.

Reach down your hand from on high—

Baracus delivered a punch to the gut....

Deliver me and rescue me from the mighty waters—

A punch to the face again. He reached down and pulled out a knife. I hadn't seen him pick up the last one, but I wasn't all that surprised. He felt that he had been toying with me before. Why cut the fun short?

From the deadly sword deliver me... There will be no breaching of walls, no going into captivity, no cry of distress in our streets.

I grabbed his wrist with my free, left hand. I locked my elbow, so my arm was straight. He was obviously stronger. He was inhumanely strong. It was insane.

"I have the power of *my* god, little man," Baracus boomed. "I have the strength of all the dead who are and were at my command. I am the dead, personified and let loose to roam the world. And who are you, little man? Just another doomed martyr to a God who has already said that my master will own the world. We shall win!"

I had only one thought left. It was one idea, and the only thing I could think of. I needed one more miracle, just one more time. I needed God to give me one very minor miracle, and technically, it wasn't even that.

Blessed is the people whose God is the Lord.

I bent my knees and jumped. I am almost certain that God kept me levitating just enough for me to bring both knees up to my chest and drop-kick both feet into Baracus' chest. I planted the soles of my shoes in his chest as I fell backwards, taking him with me. I rolled off of my back as Baracus arced above me. I let go of his wrist, and he went flying.

He flew right into the fire pit.

I lay there for a moment, my body trying to figure out if it should take a nap.

I heard a grunt and groaned. I pulled myself over to the edge of the fire pit, next to the base of the Moloch statue (it was stone in a firepit, it wasn't exactly going to turn to ash). Down the statue, between the base and the flames, was Bokor Baracus. He was still alive.

Dang it.

At least the knife had disappeared somewhere into the flames.

"Can I accept your surrender *now*?" I asked him as the flames licked at his expensive wingtips. "Or would you like to fight some more?"

Baracus gave me an evil look. "I would like to bring you with me!" he roared as he leaped for me.

In one enormous lunge, he hurled himself at me, propelled up from the statue's length, coming right for me, both hands outstretched and ready for me.

The boom of a shotgun came from my left. It blasted Baracus backwards, and he fell into the fire pit, screaming.

I didn't see him come back this time.

I looked over to where the sound came from. Alex had picked up D's shotgun. He gave me a little wave. "Do you always have to do things the hard way?"

I sighed. "No. That's why I was trying to keep him alive." I looked at D. "How's he doing?"

"He's still alive." Alex frowned. "How did you get him on board with this suicide run?"

I smiled. "D has family. He knows that you don't touch family."

Alex and I took an arm, lifted D to his feet, and carried him over to the boat.

We both got back to the backyard in time for the SWAT team to overrun the house and make it to the backyard, where we promptly identified ourselves.

Chapter 24

FALLOUT 2

After a week of tearing apart the crime scene, Internal Affairs was going to talk to me again. For the seventh day in a row. The same questions had been asked but in different order each day.

As I sat down in interrogation, I figured it had to be the final round. The Crime Scene Unit had given up on analyzing every single inch of the house. The gunmen had lawyered up at first, but as the evidence stacked up, more and more started to flip on each other, on LaObliger, and on the entire Women's Health Corps. While I couldn't be part of breaking these people, ADA Carlton had kept me apprised via text message. Apparently, thinking that one's little cult of death could bring supernatural-level amounts of success wasn't actually a case for legal insanity...if they were truly unaware of how wrong it was (or at the very least, illegal) they wouldn't have gone to such extents to keep everything a secret.

It was, once more, the Statler and Waldorf duo themselves, McNally and Horowitz.

"Just walk us through it," Horowitz told me.

I blinked. I couldn't remember the last interrogation with IA I heard of where they just let the target of the investigation ramble. But I wasn't going to let them down.

"When my son was kidnapped, I was relatively certain that someone in the Women's Health Corps was behind it. We had traced the trucks of body parts to King's Point, and that LaObliger lived there."

Horowitz asked, "How did you know it was her?"

That was more like it. "I didn't. I was relatively certain. I had been investigating the Women's Health Corps as part of the attempt on my life. You were there for that. If Jeremy wasn't with LaObliger, I didn't know where to start."

McNally followed up. "Why didn't you call in backup?"

"I did. I called my partner. If you mean why didn't I call my superior officer, I had nothing to go on. If I knocked on LaObliger's door, and nothing happened, then I would have been happy to call in everyone I know. I had no grounds. That's why I just went to her house and knocked. I didn't even need to ask to come inside. If she had denied my entry, it would have been a dead end."

Horowitz nodded. He knew I wanted to keep going. "Before we get there though, tell us about who you called in. Your reinforcements."

I shrugged. "As I said, I knew the department would have had no grounds to come with me. If I came with backup, and Jeremy wasn't there, I would have wasted man hours and resources that no one can really afford. Even in Nassau. I have some friends who own a boat. My partner had deduced that there would be a dock at the house."

"Friends who owned a lot of automatic guns?"

I shrugged and answered honestly. "The only guns used in the extraction of my son that I can say anything about are mine, my wife's, my partner's, and one shotgun, used by one Daniel David DiLeo. To my knowledge, none of the guns used that night were illegal, or illegally obtained, or even illegally used by the person firing said weapon. I honestly don't know anything about the people Mister DiLeo brought with him in the rescue attempt on my son. We were busy being shot at."

"Walk us through this plan?"

I internally flinched. I didn't want to lie, but this was going to be difficult. "I walked up and knocked. If I wasn't allowed in, game over. If I was allowed in, and wasn't out in ten minutes, they would come in and get me, because I wasn't going to just sit there and be held hostage. If I could, I would signal that they should move in."

McNally absently nodded and made a note. He didn't ask which of the two contingencies I ended up using. Either way, it would be exigent circumstances, allowing even the police to come and rescue me at that point.

He recapped. "So, you knocked. They just let you in. Obviously, because they had your son and they wanted you ... do you know why? Why did they want you?"

I shrugged. "It was some sort of revenge ploy for me foiling... something with Christopher Curran. I'm honestly not entirely clear with what's going on. The way LaObliger explained it to me, the plan involves something with demons, and worship of a Carthaginian deity. It was a little insane the way she explained it."

Again, completely true. Despite having dissected the conversation during the last week, I had no idea what LaObliger's plan with Curran was, and that they wanted revenge on me...somehow. I made certain to give them all of my confusion in my answers, deliberately obfuscating that I knew that her demons were real, on more levels than one.

"After this conversation?" McNally asked.

"They walked me out to their backyard firepit, where I found my son tied up at the base of a statue. I'm not sure if I was going to be tortured, but the end goal was going to end with Jeremy and me in the bottom of the fire pit. I delayed for as long as I could. Then Mister DiLeo's forces came in and saved the day."

Horowitz nodded. "And the bodies that were set on fire?"

This was something I had been prepared for since the SWAT team showed up to save my life... and they had arrested the remaining gunmen who had been holed up in the house. But I knew that the zombies that burst into flame would need a damn good explanation before I even left. Even though I didn't have one.

I said, "I can't exactly say for certain how they combusted in that fashion." *Perfectly true.* "I wouldn't know the mechanics of how such a thing would happen." *Also true.* "Did anyone perhaps find an incendiary device on them?" *A question, not a lie.* "Because if I were going to worship...what they did...I would see no problem with wiring my gunmen with incendiary devices in the event of their death." *Also true. But mostly a theoretical discussion.*

"Possible," McNally answered. "Now, explain what happened with President LaObliger?"

"During the firefight, LaObliger managed to close with us. While Detective Packard, Mister DiLeo, and I were returning fire, LaObliger attacked my wife. During the struggle with Mariel, LaObliger went over the edge of the fire pit."

"How did she fall, exactly?" Horowitz asked.

"Mariel shot her and struck her, causing her to fall back."

McNally cocked his head and studied me. "Do you think that your wife was still in fear of her life at that point?"

I furrowed my brows, only slightly confused. If they suddenly wanted to convict my wife of cold-blooded murder during a firefight... "She's a civilian who was not only being shot at but also being attacked by a knife-wielding maniac who had masterminded the kidnapping of her son and multiple attempts on her husband. At the time, Mariel was the only thing between LaObliger and Jeremy. If she *wasn't* in fear for her life and his, I'd be surprised."

"Can you explain how no one has been able to find LaObliger's body?" Horowitz asked.

I blinked. That was a new question. "I...have no idea. Do you know how hot the fire was? I've never worked arson. There was also a taller man who went in. I can't imagine there were body parts that survived."

McNally grimaced. "We found a refrigerator with body parts. So we don't doubt that. The surviving cultists also confirmed their 'worship' and practices."

Horowitz nodded, almost to himself, and McNally mirrored him.

Horowitz leaned forward. "Okay."

McNally shrugged. "We're done here."

I blinked. "That's it?"

McNally closed his suitcase. "Yup."

Horowitz smirked. "Have a good life."

As they rose to leave, I held up my hands. "Excuse me, I'm going to have to ask. Before, when I first arrested Curran, you two were relatively straightforward and reasonable. After Rikers, I got the impression that you two had a grudge. Even ME Holland thought you were going to press her to fabricate evidence. Now this? Seriously, what did I ever do to you two?"

They exchanged a brief glance, then shrugged as one, and looked back at me.

Horowitz sigh. "We got a note from City Hall."

McNally rolled his eyes. "They gave us the impression that you were on the take."

Horowitz scoffed. "And that Curran was a saint who may have been set up."

McNally frowned. "Probably because LaObliger was backing Curran, and she has political pull."

Horowitz glowered. "We don't like being jerked around."

McNally nodded and added, "Or being political pawns."

Horowitz lifted his case off the table. "But after this? You've answered the questions more or less the same way each time."

McNally raised a finger to emphasis his point. "Your wording was different every time you answered."

Horowitz bobbed his head. "You gave more details each time instead of fewer."

McNally nodded. "And none of these added details contradict anything or anyone else's phrasing."

Horowitz threw a hand up in the air, like an Italian shrug. "Most importantly, we can't find anything against you."

McNally tapped the briefcase with all of the files on the case. "Moreover, the guys who flipped have all insisted that LaObliger sicced Curran on you."

Horowitz chuckled. "She knew that Curran was insane and that you were too Catholic for her or something."

"She even knew that Curran could start a prison riot... Somehow." McNally shrugged.

Horowitz also shrugged. "Either way, she knew he was a monster."

McNally pointed at me. "She knew he went after you for a reason."

Horowitz caught this verbal tennis ball and smacked it back to his partner. "And her minions are happy to roll over and play dead, telling anyone who will listen that she wanted you dead because you foiled whatever she had in the works. And there are plenty of witnesses on your side."

McNally scoffed. "So screw the mayor."

I nodded slowly. "By the way, about the Mayor ..."

Chapter 25

FIGHTING CITY HALL

City Hall had summoned me again.

This time, I let Alex draft the response.

It was something along the lines of "Suck it. Talk to my PBA rep." Only there were more Fs involved.

I only arrived at City Hall after another week of negotiations. The PBA representative was a pit bull who wanted to have a chat with the police commissioner before going within rock-throwing distance of the mayor.

The week just got worse and worse for the Women's Health Corps. One of the reasons that I wanted to make certain that there was time between the shootout at the WHC mansion and my next encounter with the mayor. It had been problematic for the Mayor. He had been linked at the hip with the monstrous organization that I had been fighting. It looked like that might just drag Mayor Hoynes's political career into the same fire pit that LaObliger fell into...and whether that was charcoal or Hell, either way.

As the stories leaked out to the press, one after another, the Mayor's poll numbers started to fall. Baby body parts? Good for a 10-point drop. Demon worship? A 15-point drop. Kidnapping? Only 5-points. Rumors of trying to prevent a police officer from investigating the evil company? Another five. Trying to support MS-13 as simply "immigrants" as they shoot up several public places? That was good for another ten points.

When one starts at 50% approval, those numbers are a really bad week.

We weren't even done yet.

Against my representative's advice, a week after the Internal Affairs investigation, I deigned to meet with Mayor Hoynes. I wouldn't go into City Hall. I tried to pass it off as a power play instead of trying to avoid the stench of evil. I was still recovering from the breezes of evil, but I could at least tolerate it better outside than being submerged in it.

Hoynes came out with a swagger and fists balled, as though he were about to start swinging. I was ready for that. Today's ensemble for the Mayor included a pink shirt and a rainbow-colored LGBTQ tie and a gray suit.

I held back and didn't laugh at him.

"Nolan."

I held up a hand. "Let me stop you right there before we begin." I looked around. There were no reporters that I could see. "Before you start yelling at me, again, for the events in King's Point, I merely got a message about my kidnapped son. I made a guess about where he must have been. They let me in. I walked in without a problem. Once I confirmed that we had the right place—that they had my son and they were going to kill me—the cavalry came in. You can't really fault me for that. I didn't need a warrant, I was invited there, and I was allowed in. So... sorry about that. You can't touch me this time, sucker."

Hoynes gave an evil little smile. "You think you have me, don't you?"

I paused a moment, thinking it over. "Yes, I do."

Hoynes's eyes narrowed. "You and I need to have a long conversation."

"I'm not done."

Hoynes blinked. "Oh, really?"

"Really. Next time you decide to take it upon yourself to browbeat a working stiff of a cop over political tripe while giving political cover to those sons of bitches who gave you tons of money? You should probably make certain that the cop isn't *wearing a body camera* at the time."

Hoynes blinked, his jaw slack, as he considered everything he ranted at me in our two encounters together.

"*... the Women's Health Corps is a major provider of women's health-care in this city.*"

I raised a brow. "Last time I checked, 95% of their services were abortions."

"*Which prevents a drain on city resources,*" Hoynes answered. "*And removes a high-risk criminal element. And MS-13 is a provider of immigration to thousands of poor foreigners whose only crime is that they were born elsewhere. ... Moloch is an African deity,*" Hoynes told me. "*Going back to a great, ancient African empire! Looking into Moloch-like this is racist! How dare you. It's religious persecution! ... All rational geneticists and medical professionals know that we shouldn't allow any rights to children before they're ten years old. They were just an advanced culture, so far ahead of their time.*"

Or, of course...

"*... I told you dummies to stay away from persecuting a religious minority, and keep away from the Women's Health Corps ... LaObliger called my office to complain about your constant, endless harassment of these law-abiding citizens.*"

And I'm sure that the ACLU lawyer's quote, "*Circumcision is just as brutal, a medieval practice. His Honor concurs*" was good for whatever support he may have had left from the Jewish community.

Or, even better, Hoynes screaming, "*Enough. I'll throw you both in jail. I don't care why or what for. Then the WHC will sue you into bankruptcy over that bit of slander.*"

"I hear that it's going to make an interesting video on YouTube," I told him.

Hoynes growled, low and feral. I was tempted to look around for the angry pit bull. He tried to loom over me, but we were of equal height.

"To Hell with you, Nolan. I have more important things to do than deal with you. But remember this. I'm only in the second year of a four-year term. You can't get away from me. There's no escape. This will blow over. The attention span of New Yorkers is compatible with that of a flea. You can't believe that this will provide you cover. Even if this sparks an investigation, give it a year. It'll go away. All you will have accomplished is that you'll have wasted some of my time."

I smiled right back at him. "Then you'll have twelve fewer months for interfering in police business."

Hoynes's eyes narrowed. "Fine. I don't need this right now. I have a meeting with my Deputy Mayor for Social Justice." He turned around and stormed off for the front of City Hall.

The front door of City Hall opened, and out stepped the Deputy Mayor for Social Services ... a long and lanky black man, in an impeccable Armani suit, who I last saw falling into a fire pit in LaObliger's backyard.

Deputy Mayor Bokor Baracus.

AFTERWORD

For those who are wondering, the abortion clinic tour was actually based in large part on incidents with the Kermit Gosnell case in Pennsylvania. This includes the children who had been born, then murdered by cutting the spinal column. Also, the case of the teenager who changed her mind is another from the Gosnell case.

Also, I make references to several medical cases, several of them can be found in Mark W. Smith's *Culture of Death*. The Alfie Evans case in the UK is also true, a story from April 2018. At the moment I wrote that statement about him, he was still alive and breathing on his own, without life support—the UK doctors then decreed that he not be given food or water, so he can starve to death and get him out of their hair. He lived for nearly two days without food or water. Alfie lived for nearly a week, the hospital never letting him out of their grasp until he finally died.

And if you're wondering, one of the major Psalms used during this is Psalm 144.

ABOUT THE AUTHOR

Declan Finn lives in a part of New York City unreachable by bus or subway. Who's Who has no record of him, his family, or his education. He has been trained in hand to hand combat and weapons at the most elite schools in Long Island, and figured out nine ways to kill with a pen when he was only fifteen. He escaped a free man from Fordham University's PhD program, and has been on the run ever since. There was a brief incident where he was branded a terrorist, but only a court order can unseal those records, and really, why would you want to know?

He can be contacted at DeclanFinnInc@aol.com

You can read his read his personal blog:

http://apiusmannovel.blogspot.com

Listen to his podcast, The Catholic Geek, on Blog Talk Radio, Sunday evenings at 7:00 pm EST

ALSO BY DECLAN FINN

LOVE AT FIRST BITE

by Declan Finn

Honor At Stake

Demons Are Forever

Live and Let Bite

Good to the Last Drop

SAINT TOMMY, NYPD

by Declan Finn

Hell Spawn

Death Cult

Infernal Affairs (forthcoming)

PAXTON LOCKE

by Daniel Humphreys

Fade

Night's Black Agents

Come, Seeling Night (forthcoming)

CPSIA information can be obtained
at www.ICGtesting.com
Printed in the USA
BVHW081417300919
559809BV00009B/275/P